Llama Pajamas

Llama Pajamas

SUSAN CLYMER

A
LITTLE APPLE
PAPERBACK

SCHOLASTIC INC.
New York Toronto London Auckland Sydney

ISBN 0-590-60510-0

12 11 10   23/0

Printed in the U.S.A.   40

First Scholastic printing, May 1996

Dedicated
to all the mountains,
and flowers,
and wild animals
who share this earth
with us.

Contents

1. Dad's Crazy Idea   1
2. Molly, the Computer   7
3. Never Let a Llama Loose   12
4. The Adventure Begins   22
5. Milkshake, the Animal Trainer   30
6. Walks Silently   37
7. Second Hiking Day   46
8. Our Fourth Wilderness Day   53
9. A Scream in the Night   61
10. Stretching the Truth   68
11. Our Lightning and Thunder Day   81
12. The Stream Crossing   93
13. One Last Agreement   105

Llama Pajamas

1
Dad's Crazy Idea

My summer problems really started that morning in July when my father came inside with the travel section from the newspaper in his hands and exclaimed, "This year we are going on a llama vacation!"

"A llama vacation?!" I cried. "You mean take a trip with those one-hundred-pound furry creatures with big ears?"

Dad was already on the telephone, dialing. "Mr. Youngston? I hear you are the best in the llama business. My family and I would like to rent llamas for our hike in Colorado this summer."

Hike? I thought. This vacation was sounding worse and worse. You have to understand. My father used to backpack a lot — nine years ago, before I was born. And my mom is a pretty good day hiker on our vacations. You know, she walks 2½ miles to Grizzly Lake to look at the view with a camera and a few tasty sandwiches in her pack.

When I was a little squirt, I liked hiking, too. They'd bribe me with M&M's. They'd give me one M&M for each switchback. Switchback is the word for the way a trail climbs up a steep mountain, back and forth, like *Z*'s stacked on one another. At every turn, I got to choose one M&M, any color.

Lately, I'd settled on being with a baby-sitter at the nearest lodge instead. Oh, I liked seeing the wild animals. But I also enjoyed drinking hot chocolate in front of the big fireplace at the lodge. I guess I mostly liked crawling into my own bed at night and reading mysteries. I loved good old Kansas with our sprinkler in the backyard on hot summer days. The great outdoors was not for me.

Dad was deep into his conversation. "Llama orientation session?" I heard him say. "To learn how to handle the llamas? Sounds delightful! Can my eight-year-old daughter participate?"

That was me. I was eight years old, but I looked about six. I decided it was time to bone up on llamas, so I headed for my computer encyclopedia on CD-ROM. I inserted the disk. Next, I clicked the animal window on the monitor, then cycled through alphabetically. I wasn't certain if llama had one *l* or two. What I learned amazed me. . . .

A llama could carry up to 100 pounds — *happily*! That was twice what I weighed. Llamas are South American relatives of camels. In fact, they looked like camels without any humps. But I had a ghastly little question growing in my mind from a movie I'd seen. Don't camels *spit*?!

I wasn't sure, but I thought I remembered seeing a llama article in *Ranger Rick* last summer. The magazines were a gift from Dad, so I always flipped through them sitting on the couch in front of him. But I must admit, I mostly used them to fill up my nightstand.

I hurried to my room. My nightstand this month was decorated with hand-painted pictures of different species of butterflies. My stuffed monkey, Monk, hung off a corner by one arm. The rest of my room looked like any normal kid's room — a whale mobile over my bed, an enlarged snapshot of me being hugged by the Beast from *Beauty and the Beast* on our vacation to Disney World two years ago, my hamster cage, tons of stuffed animals, and three bookshelves.

I found the *Ranger Rick*, carried it back to the family room, and sat down in my computer chair. The pictures were a lot clearer than the one on my computer. Dad must be planning a real mountain trip,

4

complete with llamas to carry our gear. These llamas were long-eared and long-haired, too. They looked bigger than Dad — *lots* bigger than I am. I laughed when I read that bears in the wilderness have been known to turn around and run when they see llamas because llamas look so strange. The second page mentioned that llamas don't spit green goo *very often*. A person didn't need to worry unless the llama raised its head and puts its ears flat.

Dad got off the phone. "Mr. Youngston asked me why I didn't have a car big enough to carry a llama!" He chuckled. "Oh, and Milkshake, they weigh three hundred pounds, not one hundred."

My name is Sarah, but Dad has nick-named me Milkshake. — I guess because that has always been my favorite treat, even when I was a baby. "I know," I said, indicating the computer.

Dad looked impressed. Raising his right eyebrow, he clicked on the next animal in the alphabet, llangur monkey.

5

"Dad?" I asked.

"Hmmm?" he replied, glued to my computer screen.

"Have you asked Mom yet about these llamas?"

He shook his head. "Don't worry. She always *loves* my vacation ideas."

This time I wasn't so sure.

2
Molly, the Computer

For dinner that night, Dad created his famous Chinese dish, Mu Shu Chicken. Dad liked to cook during the summer — when he wasn't teaching fourth grade at Westwood View Elementary, *my* school. I was positively not looking forward to his teaching at my grade level next year, even though I knew I wouldn't be in his class. Still, he would be in charge of fourth-grade recess every morning, and he taught social studies to both sections. That meant *me*. Yikes!

Mom worked as an accountant, and she got home at exactly 5:17 every night. Dad served the Mu Shu Chicken wrapped up in big flour pancakes, so we ate with our hands. We were all a bit sticky when he brought up his vacation scheme.

"Llamas?" Mom asked, wiping her fingers on her napkin and looking fondly at Dad. "What an unusual idea, Harold."

Uh-oh. My parents must be in one of their madly-in-love stages. "Llamas *spit*," I insisted. No one heard me.

Mom took a deep breath. Then she said she would go on one condition. Dad had to *completely* take care of the llamas — every step of the trip. That way she could just hike and camp. They shook sticky hands on the agreement.

I felt cold all the way down to my toes. "Wait! *I* don't agree!"

My parents turned to look at me with their matching brown eyes. Agreeing was important in our family. Sometimes they would outvote me, but not very often. In fact, I couldn't remember it happening since school got out.

"We'll see some beautiful scenery," Dad said in his best persuading voice. "And observe wild animals. I'll bet we'll even slide on glacier snow patches." He handed me his napkin. "You have sauce on your elbows, Sarah."

I cleaned my elbows, then folded my arms stubbornly across my stomach.

"Hiking keeps you fit," Mom added. "You've been spending a lot of time in front of your computer this summer."

"Molly and I have not been spending too much time together," I exclaimed.

"Molly?" Dad asked. He raised one eyebrow. "Molly is my name for my computer," I admitted. I had just thought of the name this afternoon. After all, I'd named my stuffed animals for years. "Doesn't she seem like a Molly to you? Or do you think Computerina would be a better name?"

"You named your computer?" Mom asked.

Mom and Dad looked at each other incredulously.

"That cinches it," Dad said. "Llamas, here we come!"

And I knew I'd been outvoted for the first time all summer.

3
Never Let a Llama Loose

Ten days later, we were in the great outdoors, driving to our llama orientation session. We'd been driving since dawn. I had
to admit that so far Colorado was pretty
wonderful — the smell of pine trees, the
sound of rushing water in the streams, the
sight of the snow-covered mountains sparkling in the pink colors of early morning.
"Oh, the bear went over the mountain,"
Dad sang, his elbow resting out of his open
window.

Mom turned the car into a gravel driveway, next to a big sign that read, LLAMA WILDERNESS TREKKING. COME IN AND VISIT, YOU HEAR? There was a llama's head carved on the sign with the skinny ears perking up over the top edge.

"What an adorable sign!" Mom exclaimed. Dad hopped out of the car and Mom took his picture. That was our very first llama picture. We rolled on into the driveway. Mom stopped the car in front of a pen with three llamas. "Oohhh, they're big," she whispered, astonished.

And my mom doesn't astonish easily.

A man dressed in a plaid shirt and jeans came out of the shed. "Mr. Youngston?" Dad asked, holding out his hand.

I started to crawl out of Gray Mouse, our car. We had one of those tiny two-door types, and I shared the back with the cooler so it was a tight squeeze. I emerged as the man said, "Nope. I'm Gary. I'm handling the orientation session this morning."

I liked him immediately. Maybe it was his hair. He had a thin strand of hair braided down his neck in a rat's tail.

Mom waved her hand at the roof rack, which was almost as big as our entire car. "Our hiking supplies are up there when it's time to pack."

We had spent evenings together getting ready. Actually, Dad and I had dried fruit and bacon for ten whole days. The house had sure smelled tasty.

Gary looked up at our huge roof carrier and back at my parents with a half smile on his face. "Oh, I'll just give you the panniers when we're done here. Those are the packs the llamas carry. You can organize them tonight in your motel. Now come and meet some llamas."

I skipped toward the nearest llama, a white one whose brown head seemed to reach halfway to the sky. Gary showed me a barrel of grain in the shed and let me scoop up a double handful. Then he steered me outside and taught me how to feed the llama. "Keep your fingers flat."

The llama's lips felt soft and dry on my

palms. His ears looked so cuddly that when he finished eating, I reached up to stroke them. The animal narrowed his eyes at me, then snaked his long neck sideways right away from my hand.

"Llamas don't like having their heads touched," Gary explained.

"Do they spit?" I asked, climbing up the fence so I could rest my elbows on the top.

"Depends," Gary answered. "Some people raise llamas as pets, thinking they are cuddly and cute. And they are — for awhile. But llamas are herd animals, and pet llamas seem to think of *their* humans as part of the herd. So, when the males mature, about three years old, they like to establish their place in the herd. They start taking on the male humans in the family, knocking them around, maybe biting their ears a bit, spitting."

Dad covered one of his ears. "Ouch! That would hurt."

"Now, *our* llamas are raised as work animals and therefore don't think of humans as part of their herd," Gary said. "So they don't push us around." He ruffled my hair. "You don't need to worry about them spitting at you."

"That's a relief!" I answered.

After that, Gary started teaching Mom and Dad how to tie knots in ropes. He sent me inside to grab some cookies. When I came back out, Mom was already biting her lower lip.

"There are only two rules," Gary was saying. "Number one . . . never let a llama get loose. Number two . . . a loose llama on a rope is easier to catch than a loose llama without a rope."

That sounded simple to me.

Mom laughed — or perhaps she choked. "Surely the llamas never get away?"

"Oh, it's happened, ma'am," Gary replied.

That gave me a twisty feeling in my stomach. I get those funny feelings sometimes, and I never know quite what they mean . . . until later.

"Bring on the llamas!" Dad exclaimed. Gary gave him a thumbs-up signal and led my parents to two llamas standing nearby.

I sat down on a hill to eat my applesauce cookies. There were llamas as far as I could see, big llamas and little llamas, over one hundred of them in pens in the fields.

I stretched out in the grass. Too bad I couldn't play a computer game. I already missed Molly — or should I call her Computerina?

Dad groaned as he tried to halter his llama. The clouds seemed closer up here in the mountains. I found a wolf in the clouds — or maybe it was a moose. I hardly even heard Gary's long speech about saddling the llamas and how to pack their panniers.

"Come on, Milkshake," Dad called. "It's time to take our practice hike." Dad finally had a llama following behind him on a rope.

So did Mom. That surprised me. I could tell Mom wasn't pleased, but she looked determined. We headed up the hillside behind the ranch. Mom's llama let me pat his shoulder as I passed. He wore a saddle with a big bag attached on each side. The bags must be the panniers. My hand sank into the llama's thick fur. His name was Compo.

Compo looked down his long nose at me . . . rather like a king. "We're going to be together a whole week," I whispered. "Are we going to be friends?" He certainly had a great name. Compo reminded me of computer, of course. I tromped after Gary, watching his rat's tail bounce around on his neck.

Halfway up the hill, Mom said, "What about bears?"

"Don't worry," Gary answered. "If a bear ever comes into camp, the llamas will scream the most awful scream you've ever heard. Scares the bear right off . . . usually." He crossed a little stream. I hopped from rock to rock. Dad had to tug his llama over the stream.

Gary waited just ahead. Suddenly, he called out to my mother, "Remember, Elizabeth! Hold that rope up closer to Compo's head when you enter the stream. Some llamas —"

He never got to finish his sentence before Compo gathered his back feet under him and leaped over that stream, just like a giant deer. Mom's arm jerked up, and she sailed into the air with him. You should have seen the expression on her face. Mom's eyes were as wide as eggs, and her mouth hung open in an O. Her hair flew straight out behind her. The llama landed on the near side of the stream, right beside *me*. Mom's feet came down with a splash, and she fell face first against the llama's neck.

"You all right, Elizabeth?" Gary asked. "Compo is one of our stream hoppers."

Mom's face had turned bright red. She rubbed her nose. I could tell Dad wanted to go to her, but he had hold of a llama, too.

19

And the very first rule was that Dad couldn't let go of his llama, not for any reason!

Gary turned and kept hiking.

"What in the world have you gotten me into, Harold?!" Mom snapped.

My mom is always polite! Yet I had the sinking feeling that if I hadn't been there, she might have said something much much worse.

4
The Adventure Begins

Giant raindrops began splatting on our windshield as we stopped in front of the cabin where we would spend the night. Mom groaned, yet she opened her door and scrambled onto her seat to pop up the roof-top carrier. Then Mom tossed gear down to Dad and me — like Speedy Woman. I carried *eight* loads inside in two minutes. On my ninth load, lightning crashed. Mom shrieked wildly and raced in behind me.

Lightning is the only thing I've ever seen

that makes my mom act as if she were a scared little kid.

The packing, of course, was Dad's job. That was the agreement. Mom cooked dinner, while I jumped between the two beds, pretending I was leaping over a raging river. Dad spread all our gear out on the floor. He started dropping things into the canvas panniers, muttering, "Sleeping bags in one, the llama grain and everything we need during the day in another."

Soon the llama packs were full, but half of our stuff was still spread out on the floor. "You forgot my personal gear!" I cried, swallowing my last bite of chicken. Dad had said I could bring ten pounds of entertainment. I had chosen two mysteries, my super-duper art kit, my stuffed humpbacked whale, a deck of cards, a picture of me at the computer, a jump rope, and a harmonica.

Mom gave me a sideways look. Dad had put down his chicken sandwich and was tugging on the hair behind his ears. That meant he was frazzled.

"Why don't we go to bed?" Mom suggested, yawning. I *knew* she was pretending. "We have a big day ahead of us."

"Bed, this early?!" I exclaimed, shocked.

Sometimes you can't argue with your parents. Dad cleared off one double bed, and I crawled in with Whaley, my stuffed whale. Mom read beside me. I figured I wouldn't sleep in a million years, not with that crashing storm. I sure hoped it didn't rain cats and dogs tomorrow while we hiked. I lay there imagining yowling orange kittens and barking Great Danes coming out of the sky.

I woke up once to see Dad sitting on the panniers, bouncing up and down, muttering in a determined voice, "I *will* get them into the right shape!"

The next time I rolled over, Mom was asleep in the other bed, a pillow thrown over her head. I couldn't hear the rain

pounding anymore. The little clock between the beds showed 12:30 in bright-red numbers.

"Go back to sleep, Milkshake." Dad tucked me in, and he smiled. "All the hard work is done now."

Dad woke us up with mugs of hot chocolate and toast at 5:47. Mom and I stumbled sleepily into the car. We drove along a curvy mountain road as the sun came up. Then we bounced down a dirt track past a beaver lodge. By the time we pulled into the end-of-the-trip trailhead, I was taking deep breaths of that pine tree, Christmas smell.

A truck turned in right behind us. I could see four llama ears sticking up over the cab. The light-brown ones looked familiar. "Hey, Compo!" I yelled.

Dad hopped out and clambered onto the back of the truck. That's when I noticed that he was wearing new bright-red suspenders. They looked silly, like a clown's suspenders.

What would the other kids in the fourth grade next year say about *them*? I had a wild thought — perhaps I could find a way to hide the suspenders before school started.

"Hello, traveling companions!" Dad exclaimed to the llamas. "Ready for an adventure?"

At the same instant, both llamas raised their noses into the air and gazed in the opposite direction, away from Dad. "Ah, come on, fellows," Dad whispered. "You can be a little friendly."

Meanwhile Gary had hooked our panniers on the outside of the truck. "Everybody climb in the front!" he called. That meant I got squashed. As Gary drove, I waved good-bye to our lonely Gray Mouse in the dirt parking lot. We were doing a one-way hike, starting at another trailhead and coming out back here in *eight* long days. Gary would meet us right here to pick up the llamas.

Gary slowed down in front of the Forest

Service Station. "There's a phone inside to call me if your plans change."

A young woman in a green uniform leaned out the window of the building. "Good news! A camper picked up your llama. A cowboy, who says he *lassoed* the llama." She giggled. "We've got the llama in a pen around back."

"I'll pick him up later," Gary answered, pleased. He waved and sped up. When Dad raised an eyebrow, Gary smiled sheepishly. "Mr. Youngston lost a llama named Derby last week. It was the llama's first trip out. He pulled loose from his rope."

"Mr. Youngston lost a llama?!" Mom asked.

Mom and I stared at each other. If an expert could loose a llama, what about us?

"Now, don't you worry," Gary said. The truck hit a bump, and I bounced so high my head almost hit the ceiling. "You've got two experienced llamas, Compo and Blue Star. Remember your training, and you'll do fine."

We pulled into the new trailhead in a cloud of dust.

Our family was finally ready to start on our adventure. After loading the llamas, Gary had us pose for a picture by the Rawah Wilderness sign. Dad and Blue Star stood on one side, me in the middle, and Mom and Compo on the other side. Dad held the map in his hands, and he wore those silly red suspenders.

Later, when I looked at the picture I realized we were all grinning — even Mom.

5
Milkshake, the Animal Trainer

That first morning, I thought of myself as an animal trainer leading a great expedition. I followed the rocks along the edge of the trail and the markers on the trees. I kept my eyes "peeled for trouble," as my uncle Richard liked to say. Now, isn't that a silly saying? Why would anyone want to peel their eyes?

I balanced across fallen logs, then climbed a tree to check out the path ahead. "Lions and tigers and bears, oh my!" I chanted like Dorothy in *The Wizard of Oz*.

Dad and I liked rocks, so at noon we perched on top of a boulder, the llamas nibbling on the grass beneath us. With a flourish, Mom pulled out a plastic bag labeled LUNCH #1 in red indelible ink. Before we had left home, she had spread all the food out on the dining room table and planned every meal down to the mustard packets and salt. We ate salami, cream cheese, crackers, cookies, and fresh oranges and put powdered lemonade in our water bottles. It was delicious!

Dad gave me a whistle to wear around my neck. I was to blow the whistle three times if I got into trouble. "I can use this to lead the expedition!" I exclaimed. "Ready to move, troops?"

"Look, Harold!" Mom said, pointing upward and frowning. "Storm clouds." The first raindrop landed right on my head.

Dad scrambled off the rock. He held onto Compo's pannier and yanked out our plastic rain ponchos. At the rustling sound, Compo hopped sideways like a 300-pound frog. Dad slid ten feet down the steep hill-side with Compo, yelling, "Heyyyyyyyy!"

That's how we learned that Compo hated sudden, strange sounds.

Dad led Compo back onto the trail. Inside my green poncho, I felt like a marching elf.

Dad said thunderstorms came almost every afternoon in the mountains, so I might as well get used to hiking that way. Luckily, the thunder was distant, so Mom wasn't terrified. The llamas didn't seem to mind, either. They kept plodding along like the drip-drop of the rain on my poncho.

Soon my soft hiking boots felt like heavy bricks. So, I made up a song to lift my soggy spirits:

"My legs ache, for GOODNESS' sake!
Ooooh, OW, I wonder how . . .
I'm ever going to survive this hike?"

Mom laughed.

Just as we reached the top of the ridge, the sun burst through the clouds. I wanted to rest my jellyfish legs, but Dad made us keep walking so we'd dry out. Finally, we agreed to set up camp on a high sloping hillside past the first stream crossing. The fallen trees made *wonderful* seats.

The moment Dad tied up Compo to unload him, the llama went to the bathroom, making a pile right in the middle of our new camp. "You foul beast!" Dad exclaimed. And I think Compo understood him. I really do. The llama lifted his nose in the air and made a strange blowing sound with his lips.

Mom picked a tent site in a little grove of trees so we couldn't be seen from the trail. I set out to collect wood for our fire. The wind blew my hair away from my face. I explored the ridge and found some branches to drag back.

Just above camp, I had a wide-open view of the valley beneath me and the glacier-covered mountains rising in the distance. All I could see were my parents, the llamas, and the mountains surrounding me.

That's when I understood for the first time what wilderness meant. No buildings. No cars. No television. Not even any computers. Just us . . . my mother and father and me. And the llamas, of course.

I swallowed and squeezed my whistle, remembering what I'd chanted this morning. I didn't feel much like an animal trainer now. There weren't any tigers here, but there might be bears or mountain lions. I raced back to my parents.

"You okay, Milkshake?" Dad asked as I skidded into camp.

Nodding, I helped Dad tether the llamas. We had to screw two long, curving metal stakes deep into the rocky earth. Believe me, it was hard work. We tied the llamas out on long ropes to graze.

We ate dinner before the sun went down. At sunset, the chilly wind began blowing even harder, like a gale. I already had on my heavy jacket. "It's freezing!" I cried and dove into the tent. "What if we get blown away tonight?"

34

Mom laughed. I guess she thought I was teasing.

Dad pulled out *Swiss Family Robinson*, the read-aloud book for this trip. Mom had already read the beginning, where the family gets shipwrecked in a storm off the coast of an island. So Dad read chapter two, about them building a barrel raft and rowing to shore from the wreck.

Our tent creaked and groaned eerily, like I expected the Robinsons' raft did in the sea. The family had no idea what they would find on that island. As I drifted to sleep on my very first night *ever* sleeping in the wilderness, I understood exactly how Swiss Family Robinson felt.

6
Walks Silently

I awakened the next morning to the sound of Dad's soft snoring. "Snort . . . snort . . . bllooooow." Thank goodness he'd never fall asleep in class! The kids would tease him for sure. Then I realized I couldn't hear any wind outside . . . no creaks. No groans. We hadn't blown away in the night!

I crawled out of the tent in my pajamas and slipped on my boots to check the llamas. I shuffled out of our tent grove. I could see one proud gray head with a dark star on the forehead. Blue Star was there. What about Compo?! I ran forward into our llama's meadow and saw two stiff tan ears. "The llamas are both safe!" I yelled.

Dad groaned sleepily from the tent.

Compo was lying down, so his long neck made him only about my height. I found the bag of grain and fed Blue Star a double handful. Compo stood up nervously as I came close. His lips tickled my hands. When he finished eating, he snuffled the top of my head. I looked up at him, startled. Could this mean he was beginning to like me? He had big buck teeth on his bottom jaw and pretty, long white eyelashes. I talked to him while he chewed. "Good boy, Compo Computer. I wish I had a skinny long neck so I could be tall like you."

A stick crackled behind me. I turned to see Mom in her long underwear, taking my picture. Then I looked down and noticed that flowers surrounded my boots — hundreds of them shimmering in the sun. I spread my arms and twirled around in amazement. Compo watched me suspiciously.

Right then, Mom declared that second day a rest day. She set off gleefully with her wildflower book. After breakfast, Dad and I collected water. I held the intake tube of our filter in the deep water of the stream while Dad pumped the handle up and down. Clean drinkable water dribbled into our pan. Birds chirped around me. "What do you call a llama with a baby?" I asked, leaning against Dad's knee.

Dad ruffled my hair. "What, Milkshake?"

"A llama mama!" I exclaimed.

Dad chuckled as he filtered a water bottle for each of us. We lugged our biggest pans back to camp full of water for dinner. This sure was a harder morning chore than making my bed at home!

Dad and I moved the llamas across the stream to a fresh tasty patch of grass. Then we set off to explore. Dad wanted to climb to the top of the rocky knoll we had passed yesterday.

I had to scramble up the steep boulders, using both my hands and my feet. When I crawled, panting, up over the top of the knoll, I could see our stream in the valley way beneath me . . . looking like a curving snake. More and more mountains rose in the distance.

I imagined myself as a Native American girl who had come into the mountains to collect eagle feathers. Walks Silently — that's what my Indian name would be. I would be dressed in a deerskin dress with hundreds of beads.

Dad pointed, his eyes bright. One finger covered his lips. I stood up on my rock and leaned out into space to see. Dad slipped his arm around my waist. Right beneath us at the bottom of the knoll was a golden animal with a fluffy tail and ears that perked up!

"Coyote!" Dad whispered in my ear.

My heart pounded. I'd never seen a coyote before. The coyote didn't look very different from a dog, except that it was skinny

and very scruffy . . . maybe even *hungry*. "What if the coyote eats the llamas?!" I exclaimed loudly.

The coyote froze, then darted away into the brush.

"The llamas are safe," Dad answered, sighing. "Gary said so. Coyotes eat little animals, like mice and rabbits. You know, Sarah, I'll bet her den's underneath us in the rocks."

Why, that coyote might even have babies right now! I scrambled down the knoll to tell Mom, Dad following behind me. We found Mom reading her wildflower book, nibbling on dried cherries, with her feet in the stream. We all told coyote stories and ate a lunch of peanut butter and cream cheese on raisin bread. Food sure tasted better outside.

Soon all I could hear was the sound of the water and Dad turning pages in his book. I didn't feel like reading. Too bad my computer wasn't here. I built a rock dam in the stream. Then I floated sticks over the tiny waterfall.

We untethered the llamas and headed back to camp, Dad leading the way with Blue Star. I was creeping along in the back with Mom, pretending to be Walks Silently stalking an eagle's nest, when Compo started making a strange moaning sound. Mom patted him on the shoulder, and he didn't give her his usual kingly look.

Dad waved at us to hurry. I tiptoed toward him. "A moose," he mouthed, pointing.

Across the brushy creek, stood the biggest animal I'd ever seen. If I'd been any younger, I would have crawled right up into Dad's arms. The moose had a gigantic rack of antlers! He wasn't any farther away than the length of our hallway at home. I hid behind Dad.

Mom joined us, her knuckles white from gripping Compo's rope. "A nice, safe sighting," Dad whispered. Compo stared at the moose, moaning louder, like an upset cow. I wondered how anything that big could be considered safe. The brown moose raised his heavy head from nibbling on the brush to stare at me. Gary had told us at the beginning of the trip that moose sometimes charged people if you threatened them or bothered their babies.

My hair rose on the back of my neck. I was used to people being the most powerful, but that wasn't true here. I was used to cars being about the biggest danger. Cars wouldn't run over me out here, but a moose might!

Compo moaned again, this time a high-pitched bleat.

"I agree, fellow," Mom said and turned to lead Compo up the hill toward camp.

I stayed with Dad for a moment, then raced after Mom so fast that I surprised Compo, and he half dragged Mom up the hillside. Poor Compo must have thought I was that moose. When I caught up, I sunk my hand deep into the fur on his shoulder.

He looked down at me, and I could almost imagine him saying, "There's a monster down there at the creek!"

I figured Mom would be mad. Instead, she hugged me tightly, her eyes shining with excitement. "Isn't the wilderness marvelous?" Our arms around each other, we looked back at Dad, still standing in the same spot, as motionless as a tree.

I could suddenly see the word *wilderness* as if it were written on my computer screen. Wilderness started with the word *wild*. This land certainly was wild. I had seen a coyote and a moose, all in one day. I had a shivery feeling inside, a strong feeling. Both of the animals had given me goose bumps on my goose bumps. But they *fascinated* me, too.

So I found myself wondering . . . *What would it be like to be wild?*

7
Second Hiking Day

The bushes and flowers and trees became smaller as we trekked up toward the mountain pass the next morning. By the time the trees were so small they grew only as high as my waist, I had to lean forward into the wind to walk. My clothes plastered to the front of my body, the wind whistled past my ears. Nothing grew any taller than my boots.

I hurried forward to clutch Dad's free hand. Patches of snow appeared. I wanted to go slide, but I was afraid that if I let go of Dad, I'd get blown backward.

Dad and I struggled, step by step, up and over the pass.

Mom caught up with us, groaning, "That was *hard*."

As Mom stumbled to a stop, Compo leaned his head over Mom's shoulder and burped. Mom rolled her eyes. "Llama breath," she said. "The sweet smell of grass." Compo's ears stuck straight up and he leaned closer to her face, happily chewing with his big teeth.

"Ah, Mom, he likes you!" I exclaimed.

Dad grinned. "You two do look cute together, cheek to cheek." So that became our fourth llama picture — Mom with Compo leaning over her shoulder.

Halfway down the pass the wind died and disaster struck! Mosquitoes swarmed at us from every direction. I felt like mosquito stew. We hiked for hours, trying to find a place without them — no such luck. I slapped so many bugs that when I crawled into the tent that night, I had a horror fantasy. I imagined three giant beastly mosquitoes surrounding my bed. One of the insects was saying, "Yum, a little girl for dinner!" The three mosquitoes were all holding forks, getting ready to eat me.

I rolled over, scratched, and fell asleep.

In the black of that night, I had a real dream . . . or maybe I was still awake.

"Ouch!" a stranger exclaimed. "That was my thumb, Zeke, not the tent stake!"

Something crashed, like a bag of poles being dropped or glasses shattering. "I'm too weak to put up a tent," a younger voice whined.

"We'll eat a *big* breakfast," the man promised. "Drat! The moon went behind the clouds again. I can't see."

"Breakfast?" the kid wailed. "Pop, I'll starve by then!"

"Button your mouth," the man answered sternly. "The people who own those camels must be sleeping nearby."

And I drifted back into a deep sleep.

The next morning, I crawled out of the

tent and wandered over to the llamas to feed them their double handfuls of grain. Blue Star's lips tickled my palms, and Compo looked me right in the eye. Peacefulness seeped into me, all the way from my nose to my toes. A blue-and-gray camp robber fluttered down to land in the pine tree above me.

Just me and the wind and the animals. I yawned happily.

A black-haired head popped up behind a boulder. "Hi, I'm Zeke!"

I gasped, then stood stock-still. This was the first human I'd seen in four days other than my family, and I reacted as if he were an alien, about a ten-year-old alien.

"Scared you, didn't I?" he asked and laughed at me.

I absolutely, totally, completely hate being laughed at by other kids. All my friends know that. I stared as the boy reached down, scooped up a rock, and lobbed it at the camp robber. The bird squawked, just as shocked as I, and flew

away. My mouth must have fallen even farther open, because the boy chuckled again. He hopped down off the boulder and landed right next to me.

I found my voice. "That's cruel."

"Ah, I like animals," he said, waving one hand at the bird. He tilted his head to one side. "But isn't it funny when you get them to jump or squawk?" He rushed right on. "You going into second grade?" Before I could stop him, Zeke swaggered over and thumped Compo on the back. Compo bounded like a grasshopper to the end of his line. Zeke's eyes widened. "What's the matter? Aren't your *camels* friendly?"

I put my fists on my hips. "Number one, I'm going into *fourth* grade. Number two, they are *llamas*, not camels."

Zeke reached up to fondle Blue Star's neck. "Last night in the dark, my pop said they were camels," he said, as if that answered everything.

Blue Star narrowed his eyes and pulled his head away. He lifted his nose right up

51

into the air and flattened his ears back. That reminded me of what I had read in my *Ranger Rick* magazine at home. *Go on, Blue Star,* I thought. *Spit at him.*

"Animals always like me!" Zeke exclaimed, surprised. He folded his arms and stared at the two llamas as if they were a challenge.

"Zeke!!" a voice bellowed, loud enough to shake all the trees in the forest. "It's time to go fishing."

Zeke grinned. "Got to go." He pointed at each of the llamas. "Don't worry. I'll get these dumb beasts to like me." He waved a hand. "See ya, Short Stuff!" Then he was gone.

My dream last night hadn't been a dream at all. I sat down on a rock, twisting a strand of my hair in astonishment. This boy just might be a worse nightmare than mosquitoes.

8
Our Fourth Wilderness Day

Back at camp, Dad had a small fire crackling to heat water. He handed me a pot of warm water and a bandanna. I scrubbed halfheartedly at my arms. "Did you hear that boy and his father last night?" I asked, while Mom shampooed my hair with Willy's Wilderness Suds. "They set up camp near here. I met the boy, Zeke, this morning. He's awful!"

"How bad can he be?" Dad asked.

"You'll see," I said, shaking the water out

of my left ear. "We're bound to run across him again, sooner or later."

After our oatmeal breakfast, we headed for the lake to explore. Just behind the giant rock, we saw a blue-and-orange tent. A chipmunk happily nibbled on an open pack. The camp was a disaster! Candy bar wrappers had been dropped on the ground. An empty tuna can leaned against the campfire ring, not even scrubbed out to get rid of the smell.

Mom frowned. "Harold, won't this attract animals?"

Dad nodded. He looked worried. My mouth drooled as I counted seven candy bar wrappers, three different kinds. That must have been Zeke's breakfast. I figured I might hike half a day for some of that chocolate.

Lost Lake had flat boulders all the way around our end. Mom and I started a rock skipping contest while Dad stared longingly at the pass in the distance. I could tell he felt the same way about that pass as I felt about the candy bars.

Zeke and his dad were on the far side of the lake, fishing. Zeke waved, but I pretended I didn't see him.

"Lost Lake isn't a good name for this place," I said as I succeeded in making my rock skip four times. "After all, we found it." Mom had won the last three throws. "We should call it Bakers' Skipping Rock Resort." Baker is our last name.

Dad pulled *Swiss Family Robinson* from his backpack. The kids at school always looked forward to his reading every day after recess because he made up a different voice for every character. He read the littlest Robinson boy with a high squeaky voice.

In the story, the family was building a home in the trees. That sounded like much more fun than a normal house on the ground. I decided that if I lived in a treehouse, I would put out seeds on the railings so that the birds and squirrels might visit me in my bedroom.

When Dad finished reading, I got a great idea. "Let's tell llama jokes," I suggested. I told Mom my "llama mama" joke.

Mom sat silently for a moment. I took off my shoes to wiggle my toes in the sun. Then Mom asked, "What do you call two llamas singing?"

"Humming llamas?" I said immediately.

Even Dad didn't know the right answer.

"A llama cantata!" Mom cried.

"A *what*?" I said.

Mom explained that a cantata was a singing piece in classical music. Dad looked at her proudly.

I wanted him to look at me that way, too. I thought and thought. When I got an idea, I bounced up so fast that I accidentally lost my balance and slipped from the boulder. I splashed into the lake, gasping at the icy cold.

"What does a l-l-llama sleep in?" I squeaked. My legs stung from the cold water.

Dad couldn't stop howling at me.

"I know!" Mom cried. So we both exclaimed together, "Llama pajamas!"

Dad held on to his knees. "Can you imagine a llama wearing pajamas?!"

That got me giggling, too. The funniest part of it was that I could imagine Compo in pajamas — purple ones!

Mom pulled me out of the waist-deep water. I had goose bumps on every bit of my body, probably even my ears.

Zeke strolled into the clearing, his fishing rod over his shoulder and a finger of his other hand stuffed in the gill of a very dead fish. Zeke wasn't wearing a shirt, and he had a wreath of wildflowers around his head like those pictures on CD-ROM of ancient Greek athletes. Dad always told me to leave the wildflowers alone in the wilderness for other people to enjoy. "Hi guys!" he exclaimed. "What's so funny?"

I danced from foot to foot, making wet prints on the boulder, my teeth chattering. Dad tossed me his sweatshirt.

"Swimming good?" Zeke asked. He

dropped his fishing rod. Then he ran and dove headfirst off one of the boulders into the lake.

Mom gasped. She was big on checking out the depth of water before diving.

Zeke surfaced almost instantly, his face pure white and his eyes wide. He made fishy noises as his wildflowers floated to the surface.

"A shock, young man?" Dad asked. Zeke struggled wildly toward the shore. Dad held out a hand to haul him out. "This lake is made of melted glacier ice. The cold can take your breath away." Zeke sat on the rock, making little gasping sounds, as if he were trying to breath.

To my surprise, Dad thumped him on the shoulder. "Gutsy, aren't you?"

Dad would ground me for a week if I ever did something like that! Zeke smiled radiantly at Dad. Both of them raised their right eyebrows at the same instant.

"Jerk is more like it," I muttered.

"What, Sarah?" Dad asked.

I didn't answer.

"Zeke!!" that voice bellowed again.

Dad blinked his eyes in surprise.

Zeke brushed his wet hair back with a practiced gesture. "See ya, *Sarah*." He grabbed his pole and ugly dead fish and swaggered out of the clearing.

Dad squeezed my shoulder. "I think he's showing off for *you*, Milkshake. You've got a wild admirer."

"Aaaaaahhhhhhh!" I exclaimed, grabbing my throat and pretending to die. I couldn't think of anything worse in the whole world. Actually, I couldn't think of anything worse in all of space! "I'd rather be admired by a chipmunk," I croaked. "Or a camp robber or even a *moose*."

9

A Scream in the Night

To enjoy the view that evening, we ate our rice dinner with dried bacon by the lake. When the wind died down, the bugs came out like attacking armies. Mom and I raced back to the tent to play cards. Dad stayed out to watch the sunset.

During the third game of Crazy Eights, Zeke stuck his face against the mosquito netting in our tent. "Hey, want to come over for S'mores? We've got a great fire."

I shook my head. *Not me,* I thought.

Good old Mom said, "Sure!"

Well, I didn't want to stay in the dark tent alone. Dad strolled into camp, swatting a mosquito. He put his arm around me as we walked. I figured I could at least eat one S'more. That way, I'd get some of that chocolate.

The fire blazing in the middle of their clearing sent out flames nearly as tall as me. I gasped. Dad's mouth tightened. To my surprise, he just held his hand out to Zeke's pop.

"Welcome, welcome!" the big, burly man said.

As he sat down, Dad kicked the extra firewood farther away from the circle.

"Isn't this great?" Zeke asked, handing me a stick and some marshmallows. He squeezed in next to me. I had to admit that the giant fire completely scared off the bugs. And the S'mores tasted marvelous — hot marshmallows, melted chocolate chunks, graham crackers. I licked my fingers and reached for more marshmallows to toast.

Zeke's pop pulled a tape player out of his pack and turned on some country and western music. The love song blared so loudly that Mom winced, and he quickly turned it down.

"How about a bite of fish?" Zeke asked, holding out a piece of aluminum foil to me. "Saved it for you."

"No," I muttered. Then I added "Thanks," when I saw Mom looking at me.

Dad ate some. "Fresh fish." He sighed in happiness.

I noticed Mom secretly throwing candy wrappers in the fire. I looked around, snagged the empty tuna can, and pretended to balance it on my stick before I dropped it in the fire.

"Ah," Zeke bragged. "My pop says the wilderness can stand a little trash. There's plenty of space out here."

Zeke's dad was reaching for some firewood, so I didn't know if he'd heard.

I leaned closer to Zeke and whispered, "That's ridiculous. Hikers come out here to look at nature, not your garbage." Then I added evilly, "Llamas spit, you know."

Zeke just grinned at me. Without any warning, he hopped up and stood on his hands, beside the fire.

Mom gasped as he wobbled sideways. Zeke's dad laughed proudly, "That's my boy!"

Zeke walked halfway around the fire on his hands. I couldn't believe it! Everybody else cheered when he finished, and he flushed with pride.

But I didn't trust that boy. Not one little bit. Why, he'd burn down the wilderness, or leave trash for a visitor a hundred years from now — or he might even bother my llamas.

"Good night," I said, as cheerfully as I could manage, throwing my marshmallow stick in the flames. I faked a yawn as I stood up. Mom joined me, luckily. Walking in the dark in the woods always made me imagine coming face-to-face with a lion. At camp, we washed our hands and faces and

brushed our teeth before we went to bed. That was one of Dad's rules. There were so many bugs, I would have skipped it tonight. We put on our pajamas and left our clothes on a knapsack by our fire ring. By the time I crawled into the tent, I could hear Dad coming home.

In the middle of the night, we were all awakened by the worst sound I'd ever heard — a loud bellowing. "What's that?" I hissed.

"Maybe a moose." Dad rustled around for the flashlight.

The strange sound came again. "Aaaa-wwwwwuuuuuhhhhhh." The little hairs on my back all stood straight up.

"That's Compo!" Mom cried suddenly. "Good heavens, do you suppose Zeke's messy campsite attracted a bear?!"

That's when I remembered that Gary had said that llamas would scream if a bear came near. My stomach shriveled.

Dad sighed. "I saw a print at the far side of the lake today. I didn't want to worry you. That's why I stayed out later at sunset. I was hanging our food so a bear couldn't reach it."

Now I was glad that we didn't have a single smell of food in our tent. Compo screamed again. It sounded unearthly. "Are we safe?" I asked.

"Sure, Milkshake," Dad said. He started to unzip the tent. "I'm going out there to check on the llamas."

"No, you're not," Mom answered. "You're not going out in the dark, in the wilderness, with a bear."

I couldn't seem to breathe right. Even I knew that Dad was small for a grown man, not nearly big and strong enough to surprise a bear.

Mom sounded absolutely sure of herself. "We can live without a llama, but we can't live without you, Harold."

10
Stretching the Truth

Dad slipped out of the tent at the first sign of dawn. I stretched in my warm sleeping bag, then remembered the bear. I scrambled outside. "Dad?" I didn't want to wake up Mom, but I didn't want to wander around by myself, either.

"Over here, Sarah," Dad called softly. In the gray light, I could barely see him standing on the rock between our camp and Zeke's. I hurried closer. "It was a bear, all right." Dad showed me a footprint. I covered my mouth with my hands. I could *see* the claw marks. I peered around, my heart thumping in my chest. "Don't worry," Dad said. "He is long gone."

Zeke's tent was nestled safe and sound in the clearing beneath us, though only one of the packs was there. The fire circle looked remarkably clean, except for the shredded marshmallow bag on a rock.

"I wonder where they put their food?" Dad said. "I told them last night about hanging it." He pointed through the woods to one of our panniers, dangling safely from a high branch.

But, food wasn't what worried me the most.

I turned on my heels and headed toward the meadow where the llamas were tied. As usual, I saw the bluish-gray head first. When I entered the meadow, I *still* saw only one llama. Blue Star rested in the middle of the meadow, his feet tucked under him.

"Compo?" I whispered, my mouth suddenly as dry as sandpaper. I looked behind the trees, though I *knew* a llama couldn't hide behind those scrawny pines. My heart sank to my ankles. "Dad!!" I yelled. Even Compo's stake was gone.

Dad rushed into the meadow.

"The bear ate Compo!" I cried and burst into tears.

Dad gazed around the rocky meadow, horrified, then gathered me into his arms. "Black bears don't eat animals, Sarah, only fish and berries." He walked around, staring at the ground. "Besides, there's no sign of a disturbance here. Compo probably yanked out his stake, he was so upset."

Mom appeared behind us, still barefoot. "Harold, we have to find him."

Dad nodded. "I'm responsible for him." Then he muttered. "And that fellow's worth two thousand dollars."

"Poor Compo." Mom tiptoed gingerly across the rocky soil toward me. "What if he's still scared?!"

Dad quickly fixed a fanny pack of snacks, his rain gear, and a bag of llama grain. He said he was going to hike up the steep valley behind the lake. That way, he could get a view of the surrounding countryside . . . and find Compo.

What I couldn't understand is why he insisted on leaving Mom and me *in camp.* He didn't even take a vote. He just stalked away. That wasn't the way our family worked!

Mom just shrugged her shoulders. I climbed up the highest rock and angrily watched Dad leaving. Then I slid down the rock to face Mom. "Let's go searching the other direction."

"My idea exactly!" Mom hung the sack of breakfast food in a tree. Then she led the way. She found the stream that drained the lake and followed it downhill. "Your dad might be good at observing animals and be a fast hiker," she muttered. "But he doesn't understand llamas . . . *especially* Compo."

I wasn't sure I was supposed to hear that.

"Once Compo stops panicking," Mom said, louder, "he will take the easy route. *Down*hill. He is *not* a hard worker."

I agreed. "Compo loves food," I added.

We hopped from rock to rock as the brush got thicker. We hadn't been rock hopping for more than fifteen minutes when I thought I saw two tan ears. On the next rock, I saw a long, hairy neck sticking up in the air. Compo was eating to his heart's content in the lushest meadow I'd ever seen.

"You stay here, Sarah," Mom instructed firmly. "In case Compo tries to head back this way." Everyone was giving me orders!

Then Mom set off in a long loop, circling around the meadow. She emerged in the distance on the other side of Compo. Mom plunked down her whole bag of llama grain in the line of Compo's path. Then she sat on a rock nearby.

I'd been thinking. At our orientation session, Gary had said that all llamas are curious. He had also said that a llama on a rope is easier to catch than a loose llama. Compo started edging toward the tempting bag of grain, dragging his long rope behind him.

It was time for one of my Milkshake Schemes.

So . . . I pretended to be fascinated with something in the middle of the meadow. I raised up on tiptoes and stared, my eyes stretched wide. At the same time, I headed diagonally toward the *end* of Compo's rope.

It was the best acting I'd ever done. I hoped Mom understood what I was doing. Compo twisted his neck to look at me, then stretched to see what I was looking at. I completely ignored him.

The grass came up to my knees. I moved a few steps, narrowed my eyes to peer, and marched ahead. Compo kept glancing at my "spot" in the meadow. Yet every time he took a step toward the bag of grain, the rope slid away from me. It was horrible! When I finally got close to the end of the rope, I resisted the urge to bound. After all, Compo could play a great leaping deer and

be out of this meadow in moments.

Two more s-n-a-i-l steps, and I set my foot down firmly on the end of the rope. I wrapped that rope three times around my wrist and waved my other arm at Mom.

Mom arrived faster than a leaping llama. She gave me a giant hug. "That was worthy of one hundred hugs," she said, her eyes shining proudly. She tilted her head at Compo, her hands on her hips. "Have a nice adventure, oh wandering boy?"

Compo lifted his head to look right at Mom. Then he burped happily in her face.

I expected Mom to take the rope, but she didn't. I got to lead Compo toward camp! I felt like a famous animal trainer again.

Halfway back to camp, I heard a terrible moaning screech. I gasped. Could that be Blue Star? Had the bear come back? Mom stopped dead in her tracks.

"Let me off!" Zeke yelled. "Let me down!"

Mom ran, and Mom doesn't usually run. If I hadn't known the first rule of llamas, I would have dropped Compo's rope and followed. I tugged Compo along as fast as I could.

"You dumb camel!" Zeke screeched. "Youch!"

I stepped into the llama's meadow, still in time to see. I wouldn't have missed it for the world. Zeke lay across Blue Star's back like a sack of grain, one leg up around the llama's neck, his foot tangled in the rope. Blue Star had backed into the pine trees with their sharp little needles. I watched Zeke getting poked in the face. He threw his arms over his head.

That idiot must have tried to ride Blue Star. Zeke could have hurt the llama! Still, I had to admit, he probably didn't weigh anywhere near 100 pounds. And Blue Star was definitely getting the better of this.

"Get me down!" Zeke demanded.

Mom strode up to Blue Star and took hold of his halter. She didn't look as furious as I'd expected. But she wasn't leading Blue Star out of the trees, either.

"For heaven's sake, do something!" Zeke yelled.

Mom stood stock-still. "Have you learned anything, young man?" she asked in her steely voice.

Zeke flushed. "What?!!!"

Mom didn't answer. She didn't move, either. I thought she might be biting her lip so she wouldn't laugh, but Zeke wouldn't know that.

Zeke's eyes got big. Then he stopped struggling. The fight seemed to seep out of him. "I won't bother the llamas anymore," he whispered.

"You'll leave them completely alone?" Mom insisted.

"Yes!" he howled. "I promise!" His voice broke. "*Please*, help me."

Mom led Blue Star out of the thicket and gently untangled Zeke's feet. "How did you ever get your foot stuck like that?" she asked, teasing.

Zeke turned even redder. He was so eager

to get off that when he yanked his foot loose, he slipped headfirst off the llama. Zeke caught himself on his hands, turned a perfect somersault away from Blue Star, and raced out of the clearing without a word.

Mom and I leaned against each other and Mom laughed until she cried. "Did you see his face?" she asked. Then we tied Compo to Blue Star's stake. The llamas nibbled on the same bush, pleased to see each other.

"What do you think a llama puts after 'Sincerely' in a letter?" Mom asked, her hand resting on my shoulder.

I crossed my arms, watching our *two* llamas. "What?"

"A llama comma," Mom replied.

Mom and I made a giant celebration brunch, taking all our favorite foods, like dried apples and chocolate cookies, out of the lunch bags. We figured we deserved the treat.

As I munched a cookie, I tried to think of another word that rhymed with llama.

One of my friends was taking a fancy vacation and that gave me an idea. "What do you call a llama who loves the beach?"

Mom stirred the chicken-and-rice dish on the fire. She shrugged.

"A Bahama llama!" I cried.

Mom gave me a thumbs-up signal. "Sarah, you should make a book of these llama jokes when you get home."

I nibbled thoughtfully on a packet of M&M's I had found. Going home meant that I would have to face my other problem — being in the fourth grade with Dad. "Mom?"

"Hmmmmm?" she replied.

"When do you suppose Dad will be back?"

"No telling," Mom replied, with a little smile on her face. Dad might be the best hiker in this family, but Mom and I both knew for sure now that we were the ones who understood the llamas the best.

Dad didn't return until almost dark. He was as glad to see Compo as we were to see *him*. Dad looked so exhausted that neither of us teased him about going off on a wild goose chase. Mom offered him our leftover chicken and rice, while I told him our rescue story, just the way it had happened. I didn't leave out one single detail.

In fact, I might have exaggerated my creeping up on Compo in the meadow . . . just a microscopic bit — well, maybe a megaRAM bit.

After all, good storytellers always stretch the truth! Right?

11
Our Lightning and Thunder Day

"What do you call what happened to our family yesterday?" Dad asked while he held Blue Star so Mom could saddle him. I could tell that Mom was secretly proud the llamas seemed to like her more than Dad. We were getting an extra-early start this morning because we had to climb Grassy Pass — our hardest hike.

Nobody had answered, so Dad exclaimed, "A llama drama!"

I was too sleepy to think anything was funny. While my parents loaded Compo, I zipped down to the lake one last time. I stood on a boulder and took a deep breath. I hadn't really wanted to come on this trip, not for eight days. But now, I liked being surrounded by mountains as far as I could see. I turned in a slow circle, imprinting the lake in my mind so I wouldn't forget a bit of it when I got home.

I pretended to be Walks Silently as I crept past Zeke's tent. We hadn't seen him even once since he'd tried to ride Blue Star. I whispered, "See you when the eagle flies."

Mom and Dad and I and Blue Star and Compo trooped to the next lake. I figured the llamas thought of all five of us as their herd now. Then we began hiking *straight* up. I tied my jacket around my waist. Soon the backs of my legs ached.

Wildflowers grew so thickly on the steep slope that it was hard not to step on them — blue flowers and purple ones, pink flowers and golden ones. I smiled up at Dad. Dad looked as if he belonged here on this hillside, so tanned, with a bandanna tied around his neck, and his beard beginning to grow bushy. Suddenly, I had a horrible thought — *What if he didn't shave before school started?*

Just then, a fat brown marmot chattered from a rock above us. She looked sort of like a walking football. Two little gray ones rolled on the grass beneath her. Babies! The mother marmot whistled shrilly, like she was giving an order. The babies rushed up to snuggle against her tummy.

We struggled up over the top, into the pass. The beauty stunned all of us so much that we couldn't speak. I stared at the sunny blue sky and the green grass. From up here, I could see everywhere we'd been on our journey so far, even on the *first* day.

And I looked down on a cloud!

Then and there, I figured out that it was impossible to see this kind of beauty any other way than by hiking. The wilderness had somehow crawled under my skin and become a part of my heart — these clouds and the wildflowers and the marmots. I wanted to jump on that cloud and float over the tops of the mountain peaks.

"I'm proud of you," Dad said, ruffling my hair. "You've managed a hard hike many adults couldn't do, Malt."

"Malt?" I exclaimed. "My nickname is Milkshake!"

Dad just grinned at me.

Mom took a picture of Dad holding the llamas, one on either side of him, all three of their noses close together. The photograph would make a great addition to our collection — Dad and the llamas on Grassy Pass.

Dad and I trekked up a few more switchbacks to see Misty Lake. The high country lake looked as if a giant had thrown boulders around to make a stone path through the shallow water. Dad said we were over 12,000 feet high.

On the uphill side of the lake, we found a field of snow! Dad yelled as he slid along on his feet. I went down on my back, yelping at the icy cold, "Ai, yai, yai!" Dad

and I slid down, over and over again.

I couldn't remember another time when I'd had so much fun with Dad. I threw a snowball and hit him on the back of the neck. It was as if being in the wilderness gave him an extra light inside. He was the best dad in the world up here, even if he did wear red suspenders, and snore, and have a black-and-white bushy beard.

I found myself wishing ... *If only he could stay my dad and not be a teacher.*

Dad put a snowball on my head, then looked up over my shoulder. "Ooops, we have a wild visitor." I turned, my heart dropping toward my toes. And I was right.

Zeke was running shirtless toward us. How in the world could he *run* in this high altitude? He slid down the snow the very first time, on his feet, calling, "Hi, Sarah Bearah." He stopped in front of me in a spray of snow. "Your mom says it's time for lunch." Zeke had a butterfly drawn around his belly button with Magic Markers. I couldn't help smiling.

As we hurried back to Mom, the white clouds skidded by overhead in the wind. To my surprise, Mom waved Zeke and his pop to join us for lunch.

Zeke stuck his tongue out at Blue Star as he sat down.

"The bear got their food," Mom explained to Dad.

Zeke's pop blushed. "Much obliged, ma'am. My boy's been hungry." Zeke's eyes widened at the sight of the food, then he reached with both hands.

I looked at their packs. One of them had been tied together with sticks and rope, and the pockets were completely shredded. "Wow!" I whispered.

By the time I turned back, Zeke had already eaten half of our crackers and most of the peanut butter and two granola bars. I firmly held the bag of dried bananas, so he couldn't eat all those, too.

Dad tossed out a second lunch. Zeke opened the chunk of Parmesan cheese and ate a third of it in one bite. "I carried out our trash, Sarah," he bragged. "Just for wilderness lovers like you."

I didn't know how to answer, but I had to say something. Mom was looking at him fondly, for goodness' sake! So I offered Zeke some bananas. He took three fourths of that bag in one handful.

Dad gazed up at the sky for a long moment. The clouds behind us weren't white and wispy anymore. They were black and sliding closer, like a speeding train. Instantly, Mom began packing up.

Bits of white started sailing down from the sky.

I stood up and caught a snowflake on my tongue. Then I twirled as more and more flakes landed on my arms. It was snowing! Snowing in July!

Zeke and I both danced across the flowered tundra. He sneaked in a pat to Compo's shoulder as he twirled past.

"Hurry, Sarah," Mom's voice sounded tight, commanding. I glanced over and saw that her eyes were gigantic.

"I want to stay here forever," I answered dreamily.

"We need to move down now, Milkshake," Dad said, twisting the llamas' stake out of the ground. He handed Compo's rope to Mom. I could hear a tinge of sadness in his voice, too. "We don't want to be caught up this high in a storm. Lightning can be dangerous." I thought he said that especially for Zeke and his father.

I heard a dim *BOOM*.

"Was that thunder?!" Mom exclaimed, her voice shooting into a screech. Mom raced past Dad and Blue Star. Compo's ears flipped back onto his head. Mom was half dragging him. Dad and I followed them.

"What could be so bad about a storm?" Zeke asked. I looked over my shoulder to see him throwing peanuts up in the air and catching them in his mouth.

When we reached the edge of the pass where we would start down the other side, Mom sailed on. I skidded to a stop. I could see the first trees a *long* way beneath us.

There weren't any flowers or even grass on this side, just a rocky, craggy terrain. The trail switchbacked steeply through thousands of little rocks.

"Scree," Dad said. "Be extra careful, Sarah."

Mom was running beneath us. What I didn't understand is how she convinced Compo to go that fast.

I started down, my eyes glued to the path. If I fell, I might somersault over and over for thousands of feet. The thunder moved closer. Even *I* knew lightning wasn't safe when we were the tallest things around! As we got lower, the snow changed into a gentle rain. Dad grabbed my hand to help me go faster. He looked up at the sky, his lips tightening.

I heard scrambling sounds behind us — Zeke and his pop.

Lightning flashed over my head. At that moment, it began to pour. The sky cracked apart with a *BOOM*! only two counts after the lightning. I shivered. Mom waited beneath us among a stand of little trees. She and Compo had all the raincoats. Dad pulled me around the last switchback.

"It's too close," he said My feet hardly touched the ground, we flew so fast. A lump as big as an apple formed in my throat. Dad never worried unless there was real danger.

The lightning and thunder *FLASHED* and *CRASHED*, almost at the same instant. My teeth chattered, only half because of cold. When we reached the trees, Mom already had Compo tied up. Without even asking me, she stripped off my wet shirt, and pulled on my heavy dry jacket in less than a second. Then she wrapped me in my rain poncho and sat next to me on a low, low log.

Zeke skidded into the clearing, all crouched over like a soldier. "Don't worry," he hissed, his eyes gleaming. "I'm here to protect you." He yanked his windbreaker out of his pack, then squeezed in on my other side.

All I can say is that it's lucky I'm a Kansas kid . . . and used to terrible storms. Still, the thunder hurt my ears, over and over. Mom quivered like a leaf. Dad and Zeke's pop crouched on their boots in front of us.

"Think of it as fireworks," Zeke said when the crashing got even worse.

"Or cats and dogs fighting," I answered, remembering that first night in the cabin.

Compo began to hum, "Mmmmmm, Mmmmmmm, Mmmmmm." He wouldn't stop. That llama moaned and moaned, while the rain rolled off the hood of my poncho like a waterfall.

12
The Stream Crossing

Ages of lightning and thunder passed, and Mom stopped quivering. We walked on in the quiet rain. "I think I hear a stream," Mom said, peering at our soggy map. As we rounded a turn in the path, we all stopped and stared at white water rushing by in front of us. The rocks that stuck up were way too far apart for me to jump.

"Wow!" Zeke exclaimed.

Downstream, I saw a log to crawl on, but it was sopping wet and slippery. My knees started to shake. This was the biggest stream we'd had to cross on the entire trip! "Dad?" I whispered.

He had already started tying the llamas together, Compo in the lead, Blue Star behind. Dad pulled the long rope out of the pack and snapped it onto Compo's halter. He handed the long rope to Mom. Then Dad swung me onto his back. "Hold on *tight*."

He jumped to the first rock and balanced. As he landed on the second rock, he slid sideways. I'm afraid I nearly strangled Dad, I squeezed so tight.

"Go, man, GO!" Zeke yelled from the sidelines.

Dad groaned as his foot splashed into the stream. Then Dad began walking right into the stream in his good boots. I'd never seen him do anything like that before! He waded in icy water to his knees. Once, the rushing water splashed on my legs. Dad wobbled, muttering to himself under his breath. Finally, he strode up the other side. Zeke's pop crossed right behind us.

I'd never been so proud of my dad. He set

me down gently on the other side, though I knew his legs must be stinging from the icy cold. "Throw me the rope, Elizabeth!" he yelled.

Mom tossed the end of the llamas' line, but it came down only halfway across the stream. She hauled the rope back. Zeke reached over her shoulder to take it away, but Mom gave him her steeliest look. She threw again, harder. This time, Dad snatched the end of the rope out of the air.

"Okay, fellows!" Dad called. Rain dripped off the brim of his hat. "Let's go!" But the llamas didn't want to come. Dad tugged on the line. "Come on, Compo!!" he ordered firmly. "You're first."

Compo dug his feet into the edge of the stream and wouldn't budge. Dad leaned back on the rope with his whole body weight. Mom took a picture of him in the rain, but he didn't even notice.

Suddenly, Zeke leaped forward and swatted Blue Star on his hind end with his hat, yelling an earth-shattering "EEeejaahh!"

Blue Star rushed forward, jostling Compo.

Compo bounded into the stream. It happened so suddenly that Dad was still leaning back on the rope. He waved his arms above his head, trying to catch his balance, as his feet slipped down the bank. On his second leap, Compo nearly squashed Dad. I mean really squashed him.

"Harold!" Mom exclaimed.

Dad's face turned white. Just as he was about to slide all the way into the water, he caught his balance. Dad stood completely still, the rope clenched in his hands. I could hear him slowly counting down from twenty.

Mom balanced on the wet log on all fours, then crawled across, inch by inch. The water rumbled beneath her. She looked like a wet rat.

Dad helped her off the log and gave her a hug. "Your bravery, love, is one of the reasons I married you."

Mom leaned against his soggy shoulder. Before she could answer, Zeke leaped onto the wet log. "Now for the finale!"

"No!" Mom exclaimed in a half-strangled whisper. "That log's as slippery as ice!" I was sure Zeke didn't hear. Downstream from him, I could hear the white water rumbling and roaring. Zeke's pop just waved a hand.

Dad called out, "Undo your waist strap!"

Zeke hesitated, balanced on his toes. "Why?" He wobbled from side to side.

"If you fall, you have to be able to get out of your backpack, so you won't drown!" Dad tossed the llama's rope for *me* to hold. I couldn't believe it.

"I *never* fall," Zeke bragged, taking a step. He was so wet his windbreaker was plastered to his chest. He wore his hat at a jaunty angle. I closed one eye.

"Do it!" Dad ordered, in his best teacher's voice.

"Oh, *all right!*" Zeke released the waist strap with a quick jerk. Then he *danced* across the log.

I had an urge to race into the water and

grab hold of him. I didn't want him to get hurt, for goodness' sake.

In the middle, Zeke stopped and raised his arms by his sides again, balancing. "Ta da!" He was actually having fun! Beside me, I heard Mom gasp. All of us stared.

"Zeke!!!" his pop yelled in his booming voice. The boy flinched. "Stop showing off!"

Zeke hurried forward so quickly that his right foot slipped. He wobbled backward. Mom held her arms out to him, calling out his name. Dad splashed into the stream toward him. He took one stride closer! Then two!

Zeke caught his balance, rolling his eyes. He took another step. This time, his left foot slipped on the wet log. I watched him slip sideways, as if in slow motion. I knew I'd never forget the way his mouth opened in a soundless scream.

Both of my parents yelled. I think I did, too.

Zeke fell *away* from us toward the deeper water. His heavy pack pulled him straight

backward, spinning him around. His hat sailed off. He landed flat on his back with a splashing thump, missing a giant rock by a hand-spread.

Zeke rested motionless half under water. White water rushed over his face. He was going to drown! My own breathing stopped. If it had been anyone but Zeke, he would have died, then and there. Suddenly, he rolled to one side and yanked his arm out of the strap of his backpack. Then he yanked his other arm out.

Dad vaulted over the log. "No, Harold!" Mom yelled, but I knew Dad wouldn't stop. I gripped the llamas' rope in both hands. Zeke's pop crashed through the brush to get to the stream on the other side of the log.

Zeke tried to stand up, but he fell to his knees, choking. The water was pushing him backward. Suddenly, I couldn't hear anymore. The crashing disappeared and even my thumping heartbeat. All I could do was see.

Dad held onto the branch of the log, the

water up to his waist. He stretched forward, but his fingers didn't come anywhere near Zeke.

Mom grabbed the long end of the llamas' rope away from me and threw it. Her toss was a dead hit, thumping Zeke in the chest. Zeke fumbled with the rope. His hands must be too cold. Somehow, he wrapped it around his wrists.

Mom and I pulled him out, hand over hand. Dad started dragging himself along the log toward shore, step by slow step. The pack rolled over and over past Zeke, disappearing over a little waterfall as if it were swallowed.

Zeke's pop reached out from shore with a long arm, hooked Zeke under the arm, and hauled him into shore. "You stupid idiot!" he yelled and shook him. Zeke's mouth was open, and his eyes were like that rabbit who had gotten caught in our headlights last year.

Dad crawled out of the stream on his hands and knees. He just stayed there, his head down, gasping. Sounds had come back.

Zeke's pop clasped Zeke in his arms and hugged him, hard. He half carried him back to Mom and me. "Thank you for my son," he said humbly to Mom. Then he pushed Zeke down the trail. "We're going to find your pack!"

Zeke had started to cry, a soft gasping cry deep in his chest. His shoulders were hunched, and I would bet his teeth were chattering. He needed dry clothes.

"Hey, Zeke!" I had the sudden feeling that I might never see him again. He glanced over his shoulder. There were a million things I wanted to say, like "I'm glad you're safe," but all I managed was, "Bye!" He raised one hand in a feeble wave, then disappeared around the bend.

Compo and Blue Star hadn't budged even an inch.

Mom rushed forward to throw her arms around Dad as he knelt in the mud. She helped him to his feet. I skidded down to join my parents in their soggy hug, without letting go of the llamas' rope, of course.

"Okay, Milkshake?" Dad asked. That was like him to think of me first. I squeezed him hard. We might be covered with mud and sopping wet, but we were all safe.

Dad sighed. "Save us from beginners in the wilderness."

But I knew Zeke had learned something. I'd seen it in his eyes. And he had carried out his trash. Zeke would be different the next time he came into the wilderness. "Ah, he's not so bad," I said.

"What?!!" Dad and Mom exclaimed at the same instant.

An hour later, we set up our last camp together — in the rain, of course. We hadn't seen Zeke and his pop again. Dad had led us off the main trail up to higher altitude so we could find a private place to camp. I figured we should call ourselves the Soggy Family Bakers.

Mom hung up a tarp in the little trees, while Dad staked out the llamas and then filtered water. I tugged rocks under the tarp for seats. Mom made soup with our emergency stove, and it wasn't long before I was all toasty and warm.

I hoped Zeke was warm, too.

The rain stopped, and the sky cleared as I drank my hot chocolate. Mom read us a chapter of *Swiss Family Robinson*, about the family living in the wilderness, hunting for meat, eating bananas, and drinking coconut milk. What a life!

Dad and Mom and I sat up for a long time that night, watching the full moon rise over a mountain and slowly fill our camp with light.

13
One Last Agreement

I awakened once in the middle of the night, sneezing. For the first time on the vacation, both of my parents beat me out of the tent the next morning. I crawled out when Mom called for the third time that the oatmeal and raisins were ready. We had planned one last day hike today.

Dad was zipping up his heavy jacket. It had turned cold. "In all my days of hiking, I've never seen a sky this ominous," he muttered. The mountains above us had completely disappeared in the black clouds.

I curled up against Mom's side with my oatmeal bowl. Then I sneezed so hard that my whole body shook.

"Sarah?" Mom asked, concerned.

"I'm fine," I replied. Then I said more honestly, "My head hurts."

Dad found the first aid kit and stuck the thermometer in my mouth. "If a storm hits us at this altitude, it might snow — enough to get snowed into our tent."

That sounded like fun to me.

Mom took the thermometer out of my mouth. "One hundred and one."

Dad stood up abruptly. "You have a temperature, kid." He kissed the top of my head, then instantly became the leader. "Time to go. I don't care if it is a day early. We leave in an hour."

Dad packed Compo with a full load. That meant Blue Star only got the lunch to carry. I thought that was odd until Dad picked *me* up. He swung me up on Blue Star's back. It was the first time in my life I could ever remember being grateful that

I was as little as most six-year-olds.

Dad led Blue Star, and I got to sit up there and watch the countryside go by. Every time I felt a sneeze coming on, I would wave at Dad. He would hold Blue Star firmly so I wouldn't startle him, then I would sneeze. Blue Star's ears would always go back flat against his head for a moment.

Blue Star was a real trooper. As long as I was completely silent and didn't wiggle, he didn't mind me on his back. Mom even took a picture of me smiling, red nose and all. That became our seventh and final llama picture.

As we passed down out of the rocky crags into the forest, I started daydreaming about what I wanted for my ninth birthday. Maybe Mom and Dad would buy me Blue Star. I knew we could keep a llama in our backyard in Kansas. All my friends would love him.

Halfway down, we began passing people — more humans than we'd seen on the

whole trip. I asked each one about Zeke.

A Boy Scout leader finally said that he'd seen Zeke and his pop hiking out last night with only one pack. "That boy ate seven hot dogs!" the Scout leader said, as if he were still astonished. Mom and I smiled.

Dad swung me off Blue Star's back for lunch in a beautiful clearing, just before a shallow, *easy*, river crossing. We sat on a rock together. All I really wanted for my ninth birthday, I realized, was to know that everything was going to be okay with Dad next year at school.

I leaned up against him while I nibbled on a dried apple. "Dad?" I asked softly.

"Yep, Milkshake?" he replied.

I remembered what I had thought about on the mountain top, playing in that snow patch. "Can you just be my dad next year and not my teacher?"

"I'm not going to be your teacher," he replied, popping a piece of dried ginger into his mouth. "You know that. You'll have Ms.

Thompson." Dad looked at me more closely. "Are you worried about it?"

I was just sick enough to tell him the truth, to nod. I almost burst into tears, but that was my fever.

"You'll always be my daughter first, Sarah," Dad said, in his serious voice. "And I'll do my best not to act like your teacher very often, even during social studies." He poked me in the side. "As long as you don't turn into a chatterbox."

I grinned.

"Deal?" Dad said, holding out his hand solemnly.

"Deal," I answered, and I knew Dad and I had come to an agreement. I would be well-behaved, and Dad would treat me like he always did. I could live with that just fine. Still, that wasn't all of the problem. "Dad?"

He had been just about to take a giant bite of a triple-decker peanut butter cracker. "What, honey?"

"What if the kids make fun of you?" I whispered.

Dad put down his cracker. "Students do a little of that, don't they? I suppose they might even tease you a bit, too, about me. So . . . ignore them," Dad suggested. "They'll stop soon enough."

"Ignore them?" I asked. "When they make fun of the best dad in the world?"

Dad blushed. His ears looked a little like strawberries.

Mom laughed. "I'm sure it'll be hard, Sarah, but you'll manage. It will be good for you, learning to handle your temper when people laugh at you "

"I do not have a temper!" I exclaimed loudly. But I could feel my own face getting red.

After lunch, Dad swung me back on Blue Star's back. I felt better. Maybe it was the excitement of riding on a llama all day. Or perhaps it was the new agreement with Dad.

I said good-bye to the mountains as I rode down through the pine forest. The ground beneath Blue Star's feet changed from rocks to a sandy soil. I knew I would never forget that coyote I had seen, and the moose, and Grassy Pass, and Baker's Skipping Rock Resort, and Zeke falling off that log.

It was hard for me to imagine that I hadn't even wanted to come on this trip. And now, a part of me didn't want to leave! Every ounce of me didn't want to say good-bye to the llamas. I'd never forget riding Blue Star — not for as long as I lived.

As we neared the bottom, I thought of all the llama jokes we'd told. Why, Uncle Richard had sent me white pajamas for an early birthday present! The moment I got home, I knew exactly what I wanted to do. I would get out my fabric paints and paint llamas all over them. That way, I would have my own pair of llama pajamas!

I decided to walk the last mile out of the mountains on my own feet. After all, I'd already walked twenty-five miles on this trip. I might as well make it twenty-six.

"I'm dying to eat a hamburger," Dad half moaned. "The first restaurant we pass, I'm going to stop and get a giant hamburger, maybe two of them!"

At that moment, I saw our car in the distance. Gray Mouse! Rain started to fall. I turned around and waved to the mountains that were disappearing behind the dark black clouds. This could be a monster of a storm, especially in the high country. I guessed it really was time to go. "Goodbye, Rawah Wilderness!" I cried. "I'll be back to see you some day, when it's not snowing!"

"Me, too," Mom announced firmly. "But right now, I believe a salad would taste better to me than any delicacy I've ever eaten."

Dad grinned proudly at her, then at me.

I suddenly knew exactly what I wanted as a treat. I lifted my arms over my head, exclaiming, "I want a milkshake!"

LITTLE 🍎 APPLE®

Here are some of our favorite Little Apples.

Once you take a bite out of a Little Apple book—you'll want to read more!

Books for Kids with BIG Appetites!

☐ NA45899-X **Amber Brown Is Not a Crayon**
    Paula Danziger $2.99

☐ NA42833-0 **Catwings** Ursula K. LeGuin $3.50

☐ NA42832-2 **Catwings Return** Ursula K. LeGuin $3.50

☐ NA41821-1 **Class Clown** Johanna Hurwitz $3.50

☐ NA42400-9 **Five True Horse Stories** Margaret Davidson $3.50

☐ NA42401-7 **Five True Dog Stories** Margaret Davidson $3.50

☐ NA43868-9 **The Haunting of Grade Three**
    Grace Maccarone $3.50

☐ NA40966-2 **Rent a Third Grader** B.B. Hiller $3.50

☐ NA41944-7 **The Return of the Third Grade Ghost Hunters**
    Grace Maccarone $2.99

☐ NA47463-4 **Second Grade Friends** Miriam Cohen $3.50

☐ NA45729-2 **Striped Ice Cream** Joan M. Lexau $3.50

Available wherever you buy books...or use the coupon below.

- -

SCHOLASTIC INC., P.O. Box 7502, 2931 East McCarty Street, Jefferson City, MO 65102

Please send me the books I have checked above. I am enclosing $ _____ (please add $2.00 to cover shipping and handling). Send check or money order—no cash or C.O.D.s please.

Name_____

Address_____

City_____ State/Zip_____

Please allow four to six weeks for delivery. Offer good in the U.S.A. only. Sorry, mail orders are not available to residents of Canada. Prices subject to change.   LAP198

PONY PALS

Do you love ponies?

Be a Pony Pal®!

Anna, Pam, and Lulu want you to join them on adventures with their favorite ponies!

Order now and you get a free pony portrait bookmark and two collecting cards in all the books—for you *and* your pony pal!

☐ BBC48583-0	#1	I Want a Pony	$2.99
☐ BBC48584-9	#2	A Pony for Keeps	$2.99
☐ BBC48585-7	#3	A Pony in Trouble	$2.99
☐ BBC48586-5	#4	Give Me Back My Pony	$2.99
☐ BBC25244-5	#5	Pony to the Rescue	$2.99
☐ BBC25245-3	#6	Too Many Ponies	$2.99
☐ BBC54338-5	#7	Runaway Pony	$2.99
☐ BBC54339-3	#8	Good-bye Pony	$2.99
☐ BBC62974-3	#9	The Wild Pony	$2.99
☐ BBC62975-1	#10	Don't Hurt My Pony	$2.99
☐ BBC86597-8	#11	Circus Pony	$2.99
☐ BBC86598-6	#12	Keep Out, Pony!	$2.99
☐ BBC86600-1	#13	The Girl Who Hated Ponies	$2.99
☐ BBC86601-X	#14	Pony-Sitters	$3.50
☐ BBC86632-X	#15	The Blind Pony	$3.50
☐ BBC74210-8		Pony Pals Super Special #1:The Baby Pony	$5.99

Available wherever you buy books, or use this order form.

Send orders to Scholastic Inc., P.O. Box 7500, 2931 East McCarty Street, Jefferson City, MO 65102

Please send me the books I have checked above. I am enclosing $_____ (please add $2.00 to cover shipping and handling). Send check or money order — no cash or C.O.D.s please.

Please allow four to six weeks for delivery. Offer good in the U.S.A. only. Sorry, mail orders are not available to residents in Canada. Prices subject to change.

Name_____ Birthdate____/____/____
　　　　First　　　　　　　　　　　Last　　　　　　　　　　　M　D　Y

Address_____

City_____ State_____ Zip_____

Telephone (　　　)_____ ☐ Boy　　☐ Girl

Where did you buy this book?　☐ Bookstore　☐ Book Fair　☐ Book Club　☐ Other

PP1296

Jekyll and Heidi

Look for more books in the Goosebumps Series 2000
by R.L. Stine:

#1 Cry of the Cat
#2 Bride of the Living Dummy
#3 Creature Teacher
#4 Invasion of the Body Squeezers, Part I
#5 Invasion of the Body Squeezers, Part II
#6 I Am Your Evil Twin
#7 Revenge R Us
#8 Fright Camp
#9 Are You Terrified Yet?
#10 Headless Halloween
#11 Attack of the Graveyard Ghouls
#12 Brain Juice
#13 Return to HorrorLand

Jekyll and Heidi

AN
APPLE
PAPERBACK

SCHOLASTIC INC.
New York Toronto London Auckland Sydney
Mexico City New Delhi Hong Kong

A PARACHUTE PRESS BOOK

ISBN 0-590-68517-1

Copyright © 1999 by Parachute Press, Inc.
All rights reserved. Published by Scholastic Inc.
APPLE PAPERBACKS, SCHOLASTIC, and associated logos are trademarks and/or registered trademarks of Scholastic Inc.
GOOSEBUMPS is a registered trademark
of Parachute Press, Inc.

12 11 10 9 8 7 6 5 4 3 2 1   9/9 0 1 2 3 4/0

Printed in the U.S.A.   40

First Scholastic printing, February 1999

stared at the bus ticket in my hand and read my name over and over: Heidi Davidson. Heidi Davidson. Heidi Davidson.

I gazed at it until the words blurred in front of my eyes.

That's how I feel, I thought sadly. I feel like a blur. My life was all bright colors. But now . . . now my future is a gray, mysterious blur.

I know. I know. That sounds like something I read in a book.

But that's the way I think sometimes. I write poetry. Long, sad poems. And I write in my journal every day.

Sometimes I wish I didn't have so much to write about.

I still can't talk about what happened without

tears burning my eyes. Growing up in Springfield, my first twelve years were normal and happy.

I have wonderful memories. I don't want to lose them. I hope my journal will help me remember them forever.

Then last month, the first part of my life came to an end.

I might as well just say it. My parents . . . they were killed in a horrible car accident.

You can't imagine the shock of it. The days of crying . . . the questions that repeated and re-peated in my mind.

Why?

Why did it happen?

Sometimes I felt too overwhelmed by sadness to get out of bed. And sometimes I found myself feeling angry — angry at my parents for leaving me alone.

Where will I live now? I wondered.

Who will I be? Will I still be me?

We have such a small family.

I was sent to live with my only uncle, Dr. Palmer Jekyll. He and my aunt are divorced. He lives with his daughter, my cousin Marianna, out-side a small village in northern Vermont.

My parents and I visited Uncle Jekyll only once, when I was five. I don't remember much about that visit.

I remember Uncle Jekyll's dark, old house, an enormous mansion. I remember long halls. Big,

2

empty rooms with chairs and couches covered by dusty sheets.

I remember the bubbling, churning equipment in my uncle's lab — electrical coils, tangles of wire, shelves of glass tubes.

He's a scientist. I don't know what kind.

I remember his stern face, his skin so pale I could almost see the bone underneath it. His cold gray eyes. His long, bony hands on my shoulders, guiding me out of the lab. Gently but firmly.

"This is not a place for you, Heidi." I remember his voice, strangely high and soft, a whisper.

And what did I say to him as he led me out of his lab?

What did I say that made him laugh so hard?

Oh, yes. I raised my round, five-year-old face to him and asked, "Are you *Frankenstein?*"

He laughed so hard, a high, choking laugh. And then he told my parents, and they laughed too.

My cousin Marianna was the only one who didn't laugh.

She was five too, so shy she barely spoke a word. I remember thinking how pretty she was, with her big brown eyes and curly black hair down to her shoulders.

With my straight light brown hair and green eyes, I felt so drab and colorless next to her.

Marianna stayed in her room a lot. When she spent time with us, I found her staring at me.

3

Studying me as if I were some kind of strange zoo animal.

Why didn't she want to talk to me?

Didn't she like me?

These are some of the questions I asked myself as the bus bounced north along the narrow Vermont highway, taking me to my new life.

Outside my window, golden beams of sunlight shot through the tall, snow-covered pines. There are no billboards allowed on the roads in Vermont. It's so pretty and uncluttered here, I thought.

No billboards. And not many cars.

I sighed. I hope it isn't too boring at Uncle Jekyll's. . . .

The bus curved sharply along the narrow road. The old woman sitting in front nearly fell out of her seat. She and I were the only passengers.

Behind the endless trees, I saw a small creek that followed the road. Sunlight sparkled on its frozen surface.

My face pressed against the glass, I gazed out at the glistening light. The hum and bounce of the bus, the light on the icy creek — it kind of hypnotized me.

I didn't realize when the bus stopped. Blinking hard, I turned to the front. The old woman had vanished!

My mouth dropped open in surprise. Then I saw the open bus door and realized she had climbed out.

The driver, a big, sweaty, round-faced man, poked his head around. "Shepherd Falls," he announced. "Everybody out."

Everybody out? That was kind of funny since I was the only passenger. I pulled on my blue parka, tugged my backpack from the overhead rack, and made my way to the front.

"Is someone meeting you?" the driver asked.

I nodded. "My uncle."

He squinted at me. "No bags?"

"I sent them on ahead." I thanked him and stepped out into the sunlight and cold, fresh air. Sweet-smelling. Piney.

I turned to the bus station, a tiny white-shingled shack. No cars in the small parking lot. A sign over the narrow glass door read: GATE ONE.

I chuckled. The building was much too small for a GATE TWO.

Hoisting my backpack onto one shoulder, I made my way into the building. My back and leg muscles ached from the long ride. I tried to stretch as I walked.

"Uncle Jekyll?" I was no sure he'd be waiting inside, I called out to him.

But no. No one in the tiny station.

My heart started to pound. My hands felt cold and wet.

Take it easy, Heidi, I instructed myself.

Who *wouldn't* be nervous starting a whole new

life with people you don't know in a tiny village far from home?

The ticket window at the far wall was closed. Two long wooden benches stretched in the center of the room. No one sitting there. Someone had left a newspaper on the floor beside the front bench.

Uncle Jekyll knew I was coming, I told myself. So where is he?

What kind of a welcome is this?

I started to cough. Probably from the dust in the station. I'm very allergic to dust. My cough echoed around the empty room.

I turned and hurried back outside. Had Uncle Jekyll pulled into the parking lot?

No. No sign of him.

"I don't believe this!" I muttered to myself.

Shielding my eyes from the sun, I spotted a pay phone on the side of the station. I'd better try calling him, I decided. I dropped a quarter into the slot and punched in 4-1-1.

The Information operator had a New England accent.

"I'd like the number of Dr. Palmer Jekyll," I told her. I spelled Jekyll for her.

She mumbled something. I heard the rattle of keyboard keys.

"I'm sorry, dear," she announced. "That number is private. It's unlisted."

6

"But I'm his niece!" I protested. To my surprise, the words came out shrill and frightened.

"We're not allowed to give the number out," the operator replied gently. "I'm really sorry."

Me too, I thought bitterly. I hung up the phone.

A shadow swept over me. I jumped.

Just a bird. Some kind of blackbird, flying low over the station. I watched it land on the low picket fence that stretched behind the station. It fluttered its blue-black wings and tilted its head, watching me.

I searched the parking lot again. Empty. The straight, snow-covered road leading to the station also stood empty.

"Where *is* he?" I asked out loud. "Where?"

"Where is *who*?" a voice demanded.

uh?" I uttered a startled gasp and spun around.

I stared at a dark-haired boy about my age. He wore a brown sheepskin jacket, open to reveal a blue-and-white ski sweater pulled down over baggy jeans.

"Thank goodness!" I cried. "I thought you were the bird!"

The boy squinted at me. "Excuse me?"

I pointed to the fence. The blackbird had vanished.

I felt myself blushing. "There was a bird on the fence, and I thought it talked to me." As soon as I said it, I knew I was just making things worse.

A gust of wind ruffled the boy's thick brown hair. A smile spread over his face. "We have a lot of talking birds here. We're known for that."

We both laughed. I was starting to feel a little better.

"Are you waiting for someone?" he asked.

I nodded. "My uncle was supposed to pick me up." I glanced down the snowy road. Not a single car had passed since I arrived.

"You got off the bus?" the boy asked. He looked behind me. I think he was searching for my suitcases.

"I'm from Springfield," I told him. "I have to move here. Because ... well ..." My voice trailed off.

He introduced himself. His name was Aaron Freidus. I told him my name.

Another gust of wind shook powdery snow from the trees. I pulled my parka hood up around my head. "Aren't you in school or something?" I asked.

"It's winter break," he replied. He kicked a clump of snow. "No school."

"Are you waiting for a bus?" I asked.

He laughed. "That would be a long wait. We only get two buses a week."

"Then you just hang out here because it's so exciting?" I teased.

Aaron grinned at me. He had a really nice smile. Actually, he was kind of cute.

He pointed to the station. "My mom works the counter at the luncheonette. On the other side of the station. I'm just waiting for her to get off work,"

I gazed over his shoulder at the road, watching for Uncle Jekyll's car. "Have you lived in Shepherd Falls all your life?" I asked.

He nodded.

"Well . . . what do you do for fun?"

He shrugged. "You can go ice-skating on the creek. Do you like to ice-skate? And there's a movie theater in Conklin. That's only twenty miles away."

Oh, wow, I thought. The only movie theater is twenty miles from here!

"Do you have cable?" I asked. *Please, please —* *say you have cable here.*

"No. But a few people have satellite dishes." He sighed. "Most people can't afford them. You know, people in the village are kind of poor."

The late afternoon sun faded behind a cloud. The air grew even colder.

"I think my uncle forgot about me," I said, frowning. "Is there a taxi or something? How do I get to his house?"

"Who is your uncle?" Aaron asked.

"Dr. Palmer Jekyll."

Aaron uttered a startled gasp. His dark eyes grew wide. "Heidi!" he cried. "You're not really going to the Jekyll house — are you? Dr. Jekyll — he . . . he's a *monster!*"

I laughed.

Aaron looked so funny with his mouth open and his eyes bugging wide. Like a character in a comic book.

"Give me a break," I said.

"But — but Dr. Jekyll —" Aaron sputtered.

"I know, I know. Jekyll and Hyde," I said, shaking my head. "Dr. Jekyll drinks a potion and turns into Mr. Hyde, a hideous beast. Everyone knows that old story."

"But, Heidi —" Aaron protested.

"It's just a story. It isn't real," I insisted. "Can you imagine how many awful jokes my poor uncle has probably had to put up with — all because his name is Jekyll?"

"Listen to me! You don't understand!" Aaron screamed.

I took a step back. Why was he suddenly getting so intense?

"Just be quiet for a moment," he demanded, breathing hard. "It isn't a joke, Heidi. Some kind of frightening beast has been attacking the village. And it —"

"Give me a hint," I interrupted. "Is he big and green, and his name is Godzilla?"

I caught the hurt expression on Aaron's face, and I felt bad about my joke. "You're serious — aren't you?" I asked.

He nodded.

With the sun behind clouds, the snow-covered ground had darkened to gray. Long shadows stretched over the parking lot.

I suddenly had the strange feeling that I was in an old black-and-white movie.

I have feelings like that sometimes. I'm a poet, remember?

"There's an ugly creature," Aaron continued, his eyes locked on mine. "It terrorizes the village. I mean, it runs wild. It wrecks houses and stores. And it hurts people."

"What does that have to do with Uncle Jekyll?" I asked.

Aaron swallowed. "A lot of people here in the village believe your uncle is responsible."

"Huh?" I narrowed my eyes at him. "You're saying my uncle is some kind of . . . creature?"

"He might be," Aaron replied, his voice growing

12

shrill. "Or he might have created the creature. He's a scientist, right? Maybe ... maybe he's a *mad* scientist! Maybe he was up in his mansion doing evil experiments, and —"

"Enough!" I cried. I turned and walked away. "I know what you're doing, Aaron. It's the old let's-scare-the-new-girl gag." I spun back to him angrily. "But I'm not falling for it. *No way* I'm going to believe such a goofball story."

Again, the hurt expression creased his face. "His name is Jekyll, right?" he asked softly. "Maybe he's a great-great-grandson of the original Dr. Jekyll. Maybe —"

"But that's just a *story*!" I cried. "Do you know the difference, Aaron? There's *fiction* — and there's *nonfiction*. Dr. Jekyll is *fiction*."

"But the monster is *real*," he insisted. "Everyone in the whole county is afraid to go out at night. We only have four police officers in the village. They don't know what to do."

"They should stop watching scary movies at night," I joked. "Then they wouldn't have these nightmares."

"Fine. Okay," Aaron snapped angrily. "Don't believe me. Make jokes. But you should know this, Heidi. The villagers want your uncle arrested. The police just haven't been able to find enough proof."

"How do you know so much about the police?" I demanded.

13

"My cousin Allan is on the force," he replied. "Besides, it's a small village. Everyone knows everything around here. Even the kids."

I stared hard at him, studying his face. He seemed sincere with this monster story. But of course it was a joke. It had to be.

I shivered. "I've got to get to Uncle Jekyll's." I sighed. "Is there a taxi?"

He shook his head. "You can walk there. It's only about twenty minutes or so from here."

"Point me in the right direction," I said.

He pointed to the road. "Just follow it. It goes up through the trees. Up a pretty steep hill. But the street was plowed this morning. The snow won't be a problem. Your uncle's house is at the top of the hill."

I squinted at the trees, heavy with snow. "Does the house have a street number or anything?"

"No," Aaron replied. "But you can't miss it. It's a huge mansion. It looks like an evil castle in an old horror movie. Really."

"Yes, I kind of remember it," I said. Then I had an idea. "Can you walk me there? Can you come with me?"

Aaron lowered his eyes to the ground. "I . . . can't," he murmured. He grabbed my arm. "Please, Heidi. You understand, right? I don't want to die."

I knew Aaron was kidding me. I knew his whole story had to be some kind of joke. But why did I see so much fear in his eyes?

Was he just a good actor?

"Well, maybe I'll see you around," I said. "You know. In town. Or in school."

"Yeah. Catch you later." He turned and ran toward the bus station. He glanced back at me once, then disappeared around the back.

He's probably hurrying to tell his mom about the joke he played on the new girl in town, I decided. The two of them are probably laughing their heads off now.

I took a deep breath, tightened my parka hood over my head, and started walking. The hard-packed snow crunched under my Doc Martens.

Glittering snow-drops fell from the trees, silvery in the late afternoon sun.

"What a horrible day," I murmured. First, Uncle Jekyll doesn't show. Then I meet a kid who just wants to terrify me with a stupid joke about how my uncle is a monster. Then I have to walk all the way to his house in the freezing cold.

The narrow road sloped up a low hill through the village. I studied the small shops. A barber-shop with a snow-covered barber pole, a general store, a tiny post office with a fluttering flag over the door, a gun store with a display of hunting rifles filling the window.

This is it, I realized. The whole village. Just two blocks long.

A snowy side street curving up from the main road had rows of little houses on each side. They looked like tiny boxes, one after another.

I wondered if Aaron lived in one of those houses.

I leaned into the gusting wind and followed the road up the hill. As I left town, the woods began again. The tree branches creaked and groaned, shifting in the breeze. I heard small animals scuttling over the ground. Squirrels, I thought. Or maybe raccoons.

The road curved sharply. I still hadn't passed a single person or car. My backpack bounced on my shoulders as I climbed.

"Oh." I uttered a sharp cry as Uncle Jekyll's

house suddenly came into view. The house — it *did* look like an evil castle from an old horror movie.

Wet snow-drops from the trees blew into my eyes, blurring my vision. I wiped the snow away and stared up at the enormous dark stone mansion.

My new home.

A sob escaped my throat. I quickly swallowed it.

You're going to be fine, Heidi, I told myself. Don't start feeling sorry for yourself before you even give it a chance.

"It's an adventure," I murmured out loud.

Yes. I planned to think of my new life as an adventure.

My eyes on the house, I trudged up the steep hill. My shoes slipped in the wet snow. The wind swirled around me, roaring louder as I approached the top.

A few minutes later, I stepped into the shadow of the house. The sun seemed to disappear. I blinked in the blue-gray darkness.

And made my way onto the stone steps that led to the black wooden door. I pushed the doorbell.

Why was I shaking all over? From the cold?

I brushed wet snow-drops from the front of my parka and pushed the doorbell again.

And waited. Waited. Trembling. Breathing hard.

Finally, the heavy door creaked open.

A head poked out. A pretty girl's face ringed by long black curls.

Marianna!

"Hi —" I started.

But I didn't get another word out.

"Get away from here!" she whispered furiously. *"Get away while you can!"*

5

"Huh?" I gasped and nearly fell off the stone steps. "Marianna — what do you mean?"

Her dark eyes flashed. She opened her mouth to reply.

But she suddenly stopped.

I heard the click of footsteps approaching on the hardwood floor. Marianna turned back to the house.

A maid in a black uniform and white apron appeared. "It's my cousin Heidi," Marianna explained to the young woman.

The maid laughed. "Well, Marianna, aren't you going to let her in?"

Marianna narrowed her eyes at me, as if warning me again. Then her face went blank, no expression at all. She pulled open the heavy door and motioned for me to enter.

"This is Sylvia," Marianna said, pointing to the maid. "She will help you unpack."

"Your bags arrived two days ago," Sylvia said. "Did you walk from the station?"

I nodded. I still had my parka hood up. I tugged it down and started to unzip my coat.

"I reminded Dad this morning that you were coming," Marianna said, shaking her head. "He probably forgot."

"You must be frozen," Sylvia said, taking my coat. "I'll make something hot to drink." She hurried away, her shoes clicking on the floor.

I glanced around. Marianna and I stood in a dark entryway. High overhead, a large glass chandelier cast pale light that hardly seemed to reach the floor. The walls were papered dark green. The aroma of roasting meat filled the room.

I turned to Marianna. She was tall, at least six inches taller than me, and thin. Her black curls flowed down behind a heavy red-and-white plaid ski sweater. She wore black leggings that made her look even taller.

Again — seven years later — I felt pale and colorless standing next to her.

She crossed her arms over the front of her sweater and led me into a large living room. A fire blazed in a stone fireplace at one end. Heavy brown leather furniture faced the fireplace.

20

Enormous paintings of snowy-peaked mountain landscapes covered one wall. The curtains were pulled halfway over the front window, allowing in only a narrow rectangle of light.

"How *are* you?" I asked my cousin, forcing some enthusiasm.

"Okay," she replied flatly.

"Are you on winter break?" I asked.

She nodded. "Yeah." Her arms were still crossed tightly in front of her.

"How is Uncle Jekyll?" I tried.

"Okay, I guess," she replied, shrugging. "Real busy."

Marianna is as shy as ever, I decided.

But then I asked myself: Is she shy — or unfriendly?

I kept trying to start a conversation. "Where *is* Uncle Jekyll? Is he home?"

"He's working," Marianna replied, moving to the window. "In his lab. He can't be disturbed." She turned her back to me and stared out at the snow.

"Well . . . shouldn't I tell him I'm here?" I asked. I picked up a small blue glass bird. Some kind of hawk. I needed something to do with my hands. The glass bird was surprisingly heavy. I set it back down.

Marianna didn't answer my question.

"I walked through the village," I said. "It's pretty tiny. What do you do for fun? Where do you

21

hang out? I mean ... there *are* other kids our age, right?"

She nodded, but didn't reply. The gray light flooding in from the window made her look like a beautiful statue.

When she finally uncrossed her arms and turned to me, she had the coldest expression on her face. Cold as stone.

"Want to see your room?" she asked.

"Yes. Definitely!" I replied. I followed her to the front stairway. I slid one hand over the smooth black banister as we made the steep climb.

Marianna is just very shy, I decided. She must feel so weird, having a total stranger, someone her own age, move in with her.

"I — I hope we can be like sisters," I blurted out.

A strange, snickering laugh escaped her lips. She stopped on the stairs and turned back to me. "Sisters?"

"Well ... yeah," I replied, my heart suddenly pounding. "I know this must be kind of hard for you. I mean —"

She sneered. "Kind of hard? You don't know *anything*, Heidi."

"What do you mean?" I demanded. "Tell me."

She swept her black curls back over her shoulders and continued climbing. We reached the second floor.

I stared up and down an endless hallway of

darkly flowered wallpaper. The air felt cold and damp. Lights on torch-shaped wall sconces cast a pale glow down the hall. Most of the doors were closed.

"That's my room there," Marianna said, pointing. It appeared to be a mile away at the end of the hall. She pushed open a heavy door. "And this is your room."

I shut my eyes as I stepped inside. I knew it was going to be gross. Dark and depressing.

When I opened my eyes, I smiled in surprise. "Not bad," I murmured.

The room was totally cheerful. Afternoon sunlight poured in through airy, light curtains on two large windows. I quickly took in a single bed with my suitcases opened on it, a little wooden desk, a tall dresser, two modern-looking chairs.

Not bad at all.

One wall had floor-to-ceiling bookshelves jammed with books.

Marianna stood in the doorway watching me. "You'll probably want to take Dad's old books out and put your own stuff on the shelves," she said.

"No. I like books," I replied. "Did my computer arrive? And my CD player?"

"Not yet," Marianna replied.

I moved to the window, pushed the curtains aside, and peered out. "What a great view!" I exclaimed. "I can see all the way down the hill to the village!"

"Thrills," Marianna muttered.

I turned to face her. "Are you in a bad mood or something?"

She shrugged. "Sylvia will help you unpack your suitcases, if you want."

"No. I want to do it myself," I replied. I walked to a door next to the dresser. "Is this the closet?"

I didn't wait for her to answer. I pulled open the door and stared into an endlessly long closet with shelves and poles on both sides.

"Wow!" I exclaimed. "This is awesome! This closet is almost as big as my whole room back home!"

Back home . . .

The words caught in my throat. I was surprised by the wave of emotion that swept over me.

Tears brimmed in my eyes, and I quickly wiped them away.

I leaned into the closet so Marianna wouldn't see me cry. Get over it, Heidi, I scolded myself. *This* is your home now.

But I wasn't over it.

I wasn't over the tragedy that had changed my life, that had brought me to this strange house in this tiny New England village.

I'll *never* get over it, I thought bitterly, picturing my parents' smiling faces.

I took a couple of deep breaths. Then I stepped out of the closet. "Marianna, this closet is really —"

She wasn't there. She had vanished.

"What is her *problem*?" I asked out loud.

I moved to the bed and started pulling T-shirts and tops from the first suitcase. I carried them to the dresser and began piling them in a drawer. The dresser smelled a little mildewy. I hoped my clothes wouldn't pick up the smell.

I filled up the first drawer, then stopped. I really should say hi to Uncle Jekyll, I decided. I really should let him know that I've arrived.

Tugging down the sleeves of my sweater, I hurried out into the hall and made my way to the steps. My heart started to pound. I hadn't seen Uncle Jekyll since I was five.

Would he be happy to see me? I hope he gives me a warmer welcome than Marianna, I thought nervously.

"Heidi — where are you going?"

I turned at the sound of Marianna's voice from down the hall. She poked her head out of her room.

"Down to say hi to Uncle Jekyll," I told her.

"He's in his lab. You really shouldn't disturb him," she called.

"I'll just say hi and then hurry out," I replied.

I ran into Sylvia at the bottom of the stairs. She pointed me in the direction of my uncle's lab.

Down another long hallway. I stopped in front of the lab door.

I raised my hand to knock. But a loud noise on the other side of the door made me jerk my hand back.

It sounded like an animal grunt. A pig, maybe.

I held my breath and listened.

Another pig grunt. Followed by frightening cries. Like an animal caught in a trap. An animal in pain.

I couldn't stand it any longer.

I pushed open the door.

My uncle stood hunched over a long table with his back to me. His long white lab coat came down nearly to the floor.

He dipped his head. And I heard another squeal. Not a human cry. An animal cry.

It's true! I thought, frozen in terror.

He really is acting out the old Jekyll-Hyde story.

Uncle Jekyll drank some weird chemicals. And he turned himself into a terrifying creature!

And then as I stared at him from the doorway, he turned.

Slowly, he turned to face me.

And I uttered a horrified gasp.

couldn't help myself. My mouth dropped open as I gaped at him.

No. He wasn't a monster.

But Uncle Jekyll looked so old! So much older than how I remembered him.

My mind quickly did the math. He must be in his early forties, I figured. But his hair had turned completely white.

He had bags under his red-rimmed eyes and deep, craggy wrinkles down his cheeks. His skin was so pale and dried out, no color at all, as if he had been sick for a long time.

"Heidi?" he cried out.

He dropped the animal he had between his hands. A guinea pig, I thought. It hit the lab table with a *PLOP*. Then, squealing loudly, it jumped to the floor and scampered across the lab.

27

"Oh. Sorry," I murmured.

The animal must have been making those grunts and howls, I realized.

The surprise faded from Uncle Jekyll's face, replaced by a smile. "Heidi — you've grown! You've become a young woman! But I'd recognize you anywhere!"

He moved forward and hugged me. His skin smelled of chemicals. His cheek felt dry and scratchy.

When he backed away, his chin was quivering, and his pale gray eyes were wet.

He looks a hundred years old! I thought. What has happened to him?

His smile faded. He slapped his forehead. "I was supposed to pick you up!" he groaned.

"That's okay —" I started.

"I'm so sorry." He shook his head. His long white hair looked as if it hadn't been brushed in weeks! "My work. I'm so involved in the lab. . . ."

"A boy at the bus station gave me directions here," I told him. "It was no problem. Really. And Marianna showed me my room."

He sighed. "I've become such a mad scientist, sometimes I work in here for days and lose track of the time."

The equipment chugged and rattled behind him. I saw a wall of cages. Little white creatures, mice and guinea pigs, peered out from some of them.

I heard a long, mournful cry from a room behind the lab. It sounded like the howl of a dog.

"You're doing important work here," I said awkwardly.

He nodded. "Yes. I hope to make a major discovery soon." He sighed again. "But it has been very difficult."

He brushed a hand through the thick tufts of his white hair. His gray eyes studied me for a long moment.

"Is your room okay?" he asked. "We tried to brighten it up, to make it cheerful. This old house is a pretty gloomy place."

"The room is fine," I replied. "Marianna helped me —"

"You will be good for Marianna," Uncle Jekyll interrupted. "Marianna needs someone her age."

"She still seems so . . . quiet," I blurted out.

He nodded. "She is lonely in this big, old house with just her crazy father for company. And I spend so much time on my work. I hope you will not feel neglected, Heidi."

"No. I'll be fine —" I started.

"I hope that you and Marianna . . ." Uncle Jekyll's voice trailed off. He lowered his eyes to the floor.

"I hope so too," I said quickly. "It . . . it's like I'm starting a whole new life here, Uncle Jekyll. And I'm going to try my best to make it great."

He hugged me again. "So much trouble," he murmured. "So much sadness." When he stepped back, his chin was quivering again.

What did he mean?

Was he talking about my parents? About the accident?

Or did he mean something else? Some other kind of trouble?

I started to the door. But Uncle Jekyll's words reminded me of Aaron. And of the strange story Aaron told me.

I turned back to my uncle. "There *is* something I wanted to ask you about," I said.

Uncle Jekyll had returned to the lab table. He raised his eyes from a thick notebook. "What is it, Heidi?"

"Well . . ." I hesitated. "This boy I met at the bus station . . . He lives in the village. I think he was joking with me. You know. Teasing the new girl in town. But he told me about a beast —"

To my shock, Uncle Jekyll's pale, pale face turned a bright tomato red. "No!" he screamed. "No! *NO!*"

"Huh? I'm sorry!" I choked out, backing toward the door.

Uncle Jekyll's eyes bulged. His face darkened nearly to purple. "There's no beast!" he shrieked. "Don't listen to those crazy stories!" He slammed the table furiously with his fist. "No beast!"

"S-sorry," I stammered again.

I turned and ran out of the lab. A few seconds later, the door slammed behind me.

I stood there in the dark hallway, struggling to catch my breath. Uncle Jekyll's angry words rang in my ears. And I couldn't erase the sight of his purple face, his furious eyes, his fist pounding the table.

Why did he totally lose it like that?

Was he telling the truth? If he was, why did he have to scream?

31

Or did Aaron tell the truth? Did the beast exist? And did it live inside this house?

A hand squeezed my shoulder.

I jumped about a mile.

I turned to see Sylvia. "I'm sorry," she apologized quickly. "I didn't mean to startle you. Would you like me to help you unpack?"

"No —" I told her. And then I had to tell her what had just happened. "Uncle Jekyll freaked out. I asked him a question, and he started screaming at me."

She nodded and brought her face close enough to whisper, "Your uncle is under a great deal of pressure."

My heart was still pounding. "But he went totally ballistic!" I cried.

"He is a good man," Sylvia said softly. "But his work sometimes drives him over the edge."

I stared hard at Sylvia. What was she trying to tell me?

Over the edge?

What did that mean? That Uncle Jekyll was the beast that Aaron had warned me about?

No. No way.

Calm down, Heidi, I scolded myself. Don't let your imagination run wild.

Sylvia tucked her hands into the pockets of her white apron and led the way up the long stairway to my room. I wanted to unpack by myself. But I let her help me. I didn't feel like being alone.

When we finished, I searched for Marianna. I knocked on the door to her room. But she didn't answer.

So I explored the old house by myself for a while. Uncle Jekyll's bedroom was a few doors down from Marianna's. I found a small study, crammed with shelves of books on all four walls.

Another small bedroom was neat and cheerful. Probably a guest bedroom, I decided. I wondered if my uncle ever had guests.

Most of the other rooms on the second floor were empty, except for dust and thick cobwebs. A few rooms had furniture covered with old sheets and blankets.

Maybe I can have my own study, I thought. A little den where I can put my CD player and my computer. A place to hang out with my new friends.

New friends . . .

I wished the school was open. I felt so eager to meet some kids my age.

I moved down the long hall, pulling open doors, exploring. I pulled open the door to a small closet — and startled a tiny gray mouse. The mouse stared up at me for a second, then scampered behind a broom.

"Whoa!" I murmured. I shuddered. Are there mice in my room too?

The next room gave me an even bigger scare.

As I pulled open the door, light from the hallway swept over the wallpaper — and I gasped.

The room was bare inside, except for two small armchairs, both covered with sheets, standing side by side like ghosts in the middle of the room.

But the dark green wallpaper . . . the walls . . . the walls . . .

They were covered with scratches.

Long, deep scratch marks. Like ruts cut into the walls.

As if some animal had raked its claws over the walls . . . clawed them . . . clawed them . . . until the wallpaper on all four walls stood scratched and shredded.

An animal . . . a creature . . .

I backed out into the hall.

Heard loud breathing.

And realized I wasn't alone.

8

"**M**arianna!" I gasped.

Her dark eyes burned into mine. "Heidi, what are you looking at?"

"This room—" I choked out. "The walls... They're all scratched. The wallpaper is in shreds. As if..." I didn't finish my thought.

Marianna stared at me for a moment longer. Then she turned her eyes away. "George did that," she said softly.

"Huh? George?"

"Our cat. We had a very bad cat," she explained. "He couldn't stand to be by himself. One day, he got locked in this room by accident. And he went nuts."

I peered in at the long scratch marks. They started halfway up the wall.

How could a cat reach up that high?

How could one cat shred all four walls? And make such deep ruts?

"What happened to George?" I asked.

Marianna still had her eyes turned away. "Dad had to put the poor guy to sleep," she replied. "We had no choice. He was just too crazy."

She took my arm. "Come on, Heidi. I came to bring you down to dinner." She smiled for the first time. "A miracle is taking place tonight."

"Huh? A miracle?" I asked, following her down the stairs. "What miracle?"

"Dad is actually joining us. He usually works right through dinner. But tonight, in your honor —"

I stopped her at the bottom of the stairs. "I said something wrong when I saw him," I told her. "I think I got him angry at me."

She raised her dark eyebrows. "Angry? Dad?"

I nodded. "I met a boy at the bus station. His name is Aaron Freidus. Do you know him?"

Marianna nodded. "He goes to my school."

I glanced around the room to make sure Uncle Jekyll wasn't around. "Aaron told me a weird story," I whispered to Marianna. "A very frightening story. About a beast that's been attacking the village."

Marianna gasped and squeezed my arm. Her hand was suddenly ice-cold. "You mentioned that to my dad?"

I nodded. "And then he freaked out."

"He's very sensitive about that," Marianna whispered. "Don't worry. He wasn't angry at you. He gets angry at the villagers. They give him a lot of trouble . . . about his work. He says they make up stories because they are ignorant."

"So Aaron's story isn't true?" I asked.

She made a face. "Of course not."

She let go of my arm and led the way to the dining room. Outside the front window, I saw a bright half moon rising over the bare trees. The tree branches bent and swayed. Wind rattled the old windowpanes.

The dining room was bright and cheerful. A crystal chandelier sent sparkly light down over the long, white-tableclothed table.

Uncle Jekyll was already seated at the head of the table. He had removed his lab coat. He wore a blue denim work shirt over khakis. His thick white hair had been slicked down.

He smiled as Marianna and I entered the room. Then he motioned with his big hands for us to take our seats across from each other. "Where were you? Heidi, I hope you didn't get lost."

"No. Marianna is a good guide," I said. "But this house would be easy to get lost in," I added.

He patted my hand. "Don't worry. You'll learn your way around quickly."

Sylvia brought in steaming bowls of chowder.

"This is real New England clam chowder," Uncle Jekyll said, lowering his head to the bowl

37

and inhaling the steam. "Look at all those clams. Bet you didn't have chowder like this in Springfield."

I laughed. "No. Our chowder came from a can."

My uncle's good mood, the bright, sparkly room, and the wonderful aroma of the creamy, thick chowder were helping to cheer me up.

We had a very pleasant dinner. Uncle Jekyll did most of the talking. Marianna ate silently and only spoke when asked a question. But I was beginning to feel a lot more comfortable, a lot more welcome.

As we ate dessert — warm apple pie with vanilla ice cream — Uncle Jekyll recalled my last visit. He told once again the story of how I asked him if he was Frankenstein.

He and I laughed all over again. Marianna ate her dessert silently, eyes lowered.

"You thought I was a mad scientist even then," he said, grinning, his silvery-gray eyes sparkling in the chandelier light. "And, of course, you were right!" he joked.

"If your name is Jekyll, you have no choice," my uncle continued, swallowing a big spoonful of ice cream. "You have to be a mad scientist. People expect it of you. I guess if I wasn't a scientist —"

"Dad, please —" Marianna interrupted. Bright pink circles had erupted on her cheeks. She appeared embarrassed by what he was saying.

Uncle Jekyll ignored her. He waved his spoon in the air. "I think the original Dr. Jekyll got a bum rap," he continued. "Everyone thought he was a villain. But Dr. Jekyll was actually a brilliant scientist."

I laughed. "A brilliant scientist? I thought he drank stuff that turned him into an evil beast."

Uncle Jekyll nodded. "But you have to be *brilliant* to invent a formula that will change a person so completely. Can you *imagine* finding such an exciting formula?"

"Dad — please!" Marianna begged. "Do we really have to talk about this?"

"Of course we have pills today that change people," he continued. "We have pills to make you sleepy, pills to make you calm. But imagine if someone invented something that totally changed your *whole* personality. That changed you into an entirely different creature! Wow!"

Across the table from me, Marianna gritted her teeth angrily. "Dad — if you don't change the subject . . ."

"Okay, okay." He raised his huge, bony hands in surrender. "But I still think the original Dr. Jekyll was misunderstood."

Later that night, I thought about our dinner conversation as I got ready for bed. Why had it upset Marianna so much? I wondered.

At first, she had seemed embarrassed. Then she became angry.

She definitely didn't want her dad to talk about

strange formulas that totally changed people. Why not? Because it frightened her?

Or because she knows a secret? A secret about her dad. About the mysterious work he is doing in his lab.

No, Heidi. I scolded myself again. Don't jump to crazy conclusions. Forget about Aaron's dumb story.

I shivered as I pulled on a flannel nightshirt. My room was cold and drafty. But I moved to the window and pulled it open a few inches.

Even in the winter I can't sleep with the bedroom window closed. I have to have fresh air.

A cold breeze fluttered the curtains around me. I backed away from them, turned off the lamp on my bed table, and climbed under the heavy quilt on my bed.

My first night in my new room.

The sheets felt scratchy. And the heavy quilt smelled of mothballs.

Shivering, I pulled the quilt up to my chin and waited to warm up. Silvery moonlight washed in through the window. The curtains fluttered softly.

I shut my eyes and tried to clear my mind.

So much had happened to me. So many changes. So much to think about.

I knew it would take me a long time to fall asleep. No matter how hard I tried, I couldn't shut off my mind.

The faces of my friends back in Springfield

floated in front of me. Then I saw my parents, looking so healthy, so happy. I saw my school... the house I grew up in...

I thought about my bus ride. About Aaron.

About Marianna's strange, unfriendly greeting at the front door...

Faces... pictures... so many words...

I was just drifting off to sleep when the terrifying screams began.

I sat straight up, my heart pounding.

Another high, shrill scream.

From right outside my window?

I kicked off the heavy quilt and started to climb out of bed. My legs were tangled in the sheet, and I nearly fell.

The curtains fluttered over me as I dove to the open window and peered out. No one near the house.

The screams were coming from the village.

Gazing down the hill, I saw flashing lights in the town. I heard the wail of sirens, rising and falling. And I saw people running between the houses, running down the main street. Running in small groups.

Dogs barked. I heard a man shouting frantically

through a loudspeaker, but I couldn't make out the words.

"It's like a bad dream," I murmured out loud.

I shivered as the cold seeped through my night-shirt. Blown by the strong, steady breeze, the window curtains swirled behind me.

I backed away from the window, the screams and siren wails still in my ears. I hugged myself, trying to warm up.

What is going on down there? I wondered.

My first thought was that a fire had broken out. But I hadn't seen any flames.

And then I remembered Aaron's story. "We're all afraid to go out at night," he told me, his dark, serious eyes burning into mine.

The beast?

Was there really a beast out there?

Uncle Jekyll insisted that the beast didn't exist. He had acted so strange, so angry when I mentioned it.

If there was no beast, no wild, evil creature that attacked the town — what was happening down there?

My mind spinning, I lurched to my closet. I searched in the dark for my robe.

I'm going downstairs and asking Uncle Jekyll to explain, I decided.

The sirens. The flashing lights. The screaming people running from their homes.

It really is like a bad dream. Except I know I'm awake.

"Aaaagh!" I let out a frustrated cry. I couldn't find my robe. Had I unpacked it? This new room — this new closet — I didn't know where anything was!

A sob escaped my throat. Will I ever feel at home here? I wondered.

How can I feel at home when there's a *horror movie* going on outside my window?

I had tossed my jeans and sweatshirt on the chair beside my dresser. I pulled them on quickly, my hands trembling, and hurried into the hall.

A single ceiling light near Marianna's room at the end of the hall cast a dim circle of light. Squinting until my eyes adjusted, I ran to Uncle Jekyll's room.

The door stood half open. I knocked and called his name.

No answer.

I pushed the door open and peered inside. "Uncle Jekyll?"

No. Not there. The bed was still made. He hadn't come up to sleep yet.

"He must still be in his lab," I murmured to myself. Marianna said that he worked all hours of the night.

I turned and hurried down the stairs. Then I made my way along the back hall till I came to my uncle's lab.

"Uncle Jekyll? Are you in there?"

The door stood open. Pale fluorescent light washed down from low ceiling lamps, making everything look an eerie green.

I poked my head in. "Uncle Jekyll?"

The equipment bubbled and churned. A row of small red lights on a machine in the corner blinked on and off.

I stepped into the lab. A sharp, sour aroma greeted my nose. On the long lab table, a thick green liquid dripped slowly — one drip at a time — from a high glass tube into a large glass beaker.

"Uncle Jekyll? Are you in here?"

I made my way along the table and peered into the little room behind the lab. No. No sign of him.

I turned to leave. But stopped when my eyes landed on the object at the edge of the table.

A drinking glass. Empty except for a little puddle on the bottom and a green film on the sides.

I swallowed hard and stepped up to examine the glass. I stared into it. Then I sniffed it. It smelled sharp and sour.

"Ugh." I backed away.

The thick green liquid clung to the sides. Was it the same liquid dripping from the glass tube?

Did my uncle drink that stuff?

Did he drink that foul liquid and turn himself into a creature, a wild beast? Was he down in the village now, attacking people, terrifying everyone?

45

"That's crazy!" I cried. My voice echoed shrilly off the walls of the lab.

The red lights blinked on and off. And the *DRIP DRIP DRIP* of the thick green liquid into the glass beaker seemed to grow louder.

I don't *want* to live in a horror movie! I told myself.

I covered my ears with my hands. I couldn't stand the blinking lights, the bubbling, churning, and dripping.

I ran out of the lab. Down the back hall, searching every room for him. The kitchen. The dining room. A den I hadn't seen yet. The living room.

Dark. All dark.

No sign of Uncle Jekyll.

If he wasn't down in the village, terrorizing everyone, *where was he*?

I stopped at the front stairs, breathing hard. I leaned on the smooth wood of the banister, waiting to catch my breath.

And then my entire body went cold — and I froze in fright as the heavy front door creaked and swung open.

10

I gripped the banister and gaped in silence as Uncle Jekyll staggered into the house.

His white hair shot out wildly around his head, as if it had been shocked with electricity. His pale eyes bulged. His face was smeared with dirt.

He didn't see me. He shut his eyes tight as if he were in pain. He uttered a low groan as he bumped the door closed with his shoulder.

The sleeve of his black overcoat was ripped at the shoulder. His blue work shirt had come untucked from his pants. Long, muddy smears ran down the front of the shirt. Most of the buttons were missing.

Wheezing loudly, Uncle Jekyll lurched across the front entryway. His boots left a trail of muddy prints on the floor. The legs of his pants were stained, one knee torn.

I gripped the banister tighter. I wanted to disappear. I didn't want him to see me there. I didn't want him to explain where he had been or what he had done.

I didn't want to know.

It was all too terrifying.

"Heidi —"

I shuddered when he rasped my name. I squeezed the banister so hard my hand ached.

"Heidi? What are you doing down here?" he demanded, moving closer, eyeing me warily.

"I — I couldn't sleep," I choked out. "I heard noises. Screams and things."

He tried to push down his hair, but it remained wild and standing straight up. His pale gray eyes searched my face, as if trying to see inside me, to find out what I knew. What I suspected.

"Uncle Jekyll —" I said in a trembling voice. "Where did you go?"

"For a walk," he answered quickly. He scratched his cheek. "I like the air late at night. I often take a long walk around the hill when I have finished my work."

"But your clothes —" I started to protest. "Your face —"

"I fell," he answered quickly. A strange smile spread over his mud-smeared face. "I must look a sight. Sorry if I frightened you, Heidi."

"You . . . fell?" My eyes went to the missing buttons on his shirt, the tear at the knee of his pants.

He nodded. "The tall grass is so slick after a heavy frost," he said. "I wasn't watching where I was going. I was foolish. I usually bring my flashlight, but tonight I forgot it."

"And you fell? Are you hurt?" I asked.

He sighed. "Not too bad. My head hit a low branch. I couldn't see it in the dark." He rubbed his forehead. "I was so startled, I slipped and rolled halfway down the hill."

"That's awful," I declared.

Did I believe him?

I wanted to. I really wanted to.

But I didn't.

He rubbed his forehead some more. His eyes remained locked on me. "Next time I'll remember the flashlight," he said. "I could have broken my neck."

"I — I heard screams," I stammered. "From the village. I saw lights and heard sirens. I —"

"I don't know what that is," he replied sharply.

"Something bad —" I started. "People were running and —"

"I didn't see anything," he interrupted. "I was walking in the woods. I couldn't see the village. I didn't hear anything."

"It was so frightening," I told him. "The screams woke me up."

He shook his head and rubbed the back of his neck. "I'm so sorry," he murmured. The tenderness in his voice took me by surprise.

"It's your first day here," he continued. "I know how hard this is for you. I know your whole life has been turned upside down, Heidi."

"Yes," I agreed. I lowered my head so he couldn't see the tears brimming in my eyes.

"Give yourself time to adjust," Uncle Jekyll advised, speaking in a whisper. "These tiny New England villages can be a little strange. Try not to pay attention. Try to let things slide for a while. You'll be a lot happier if you do."

Let things slide?

Don't pay attention?

What was he saying? That I should *ignore* the screams and sirens and people running wildly through the town?

I stared hard at him, trying to understand.

He said I'd be a lot happier if I ignored what I heard and saw.

Was that advice from a caring uncle?

Or a threat?

It took a long time to get back to sleep. The excitement had ended down in the town. No more sirens or screams. A few dogs continued to bark. But all else was silent.

I pulled the quilt up high and stared at the ceiling. My mind spun with thoughts of all that had happened.

Uncle Jekyll was lying to me. I knew that.

He hadn't fallen down the hill. And he knew very well what had happened in town.

But was he lying to protect me? Or to protect himself?

Finally, I fell into a deep, dreamless sleep.

I slept late. When I awoke and went to the window, the sun was already high over the winter-bare trees. The snow down the hill sparkled brightly. For a brief second, I glimpsed a deer trotting into a thick cluster of pines.

I stretched, smiling as the fresh morning air floated in through my open window. But my good mood vanished as soon as the frightening memory of the night before swept back into my mind.

I have to know the truth, I told myself.

I won't be able to relax — until I learn the truth about Uncle Jekyll.

I pulled on a clean pair of black leggings and a bright yellow wool sweater and hurried down to breakfast.

But angry, shouting voices made me stop in the hall outside the kitchen.

"I don't have to stay here!" I heard Marianna cry angrily. "I don't have to live like this!"

"Sure, sure," Uncle Jekyll replied sarcastically. "And where would you go?"

"Anywhere!" she shrieked. "Anywhere where I didn't have to put up with you!"

"Keep your voice down," Uncle Jekyll urged, sounding desperate. "The whole house doesn't have to hear."

"I don't care! I really don't care!" Marianna wailed. "I'm so tired of living with so many lies, so many secrets! I — I can't do it anymore, Dad! You're asking too much!"

Leaning against the wall, out of sight of the kitchen door, I clapped my hand over my mouth to keep from gasping.

What was Marianna saying? Did she know the truth about her father?

My heart pounded as I eavesdropped on their argument.

"I can't have any friends," Marianna was saying in a trembling, emotional voice. "I can't invite anyone over. I have no life, Dad. No life at all. And it's all your fault!"

"You have to be patient," Uncle Jekyll replied heatedly. "You have to give me time, Marianna. You know it isn't my fault."

"I don't care!" she shrieked. "I don't care anymore!"

Uncle Jekyll started to say something else. But I coughed. I didn't even realize I had done it.

Their argument ended instantly. The kitchen was silent now.

I took a deep breath. Put a blank expression on my face. And tried to act casual as I walked into the room.

Everyone said good morning.

Uncle Jekyll smiled. But Marianna gritted her teeth and glanced away.

Her bowl of cereal hadn't been touched. Her dark curls fell damply over her face. Her hands were clenched into tight fists on the table-top.

"Would you like some eggs?" Uncle Jekyll asked, the smile plastered on his face. "Sylvia can make them for you any way you like."

"No. I'll just have cereal." I reached across the table for the box. "I'm not a big breakfast person."

"Marianna and I were just having a little family discussion," Uncle Jekyll said, grinning across the table at her.

Marianna scowled and didn't raise her eyes.

"Oh, really?" I said. "I missed it."

No one said much for the rest of breakfast. I couldn't wait to take Marianna aside and find out what she knew. I'm not going to let her go until she tells me everything, I vowed.

After breakfast, Uncle Jekyll disappeared into his lab. He closed the door after him, and then I heard him lock it.

I tracked Marianna down in her room. She was leaning over a small glass cage. She held a cute brown-and-white hamster in her hand.

"Who is that?" I asked, trying to sound cheerful and bright.

"Ernie," Marianna replied, not turning around. The hamster moved from hand to hand. "Ernie is my best friend in the whole world."

"He's cute," I said. I stepped up beside her. "I like his pink nose."

Marianna nodded but didn't reply.

I took a deep breath. I couldn't wait any longer. I had to hear her story.

"I lied this morning," I confessed. "Before breakfast. I heard you and your dad."

She wrapped Ernie in one hand. Her dark eyes flashed. "You did?"

I nodded. "You sounded pretty steamed."

Marianna frowned. "We were just talking. You know."

"No, you weren't," I blurted out. "I heard what you were saying. About lies and secrets."

She didn't reply. She narrowed her eyes at me thoughtfully. "No big deal," she murmured.

"Come on, Marianna," I pleaded. "Tell me the truth. I heard the screams from the town last night. From my bedroom window, I can see everything down there. I heard the sirens. I saw the people running."

"I . . . I don't know anything about that," she murmured.

"Yes, you do!" I insisted. "I want to know the truth, Marianna. The truth about your dad. You have to tell me. You have to!"

Marianna staggered back. Her face contorted angrily. "Leave me alone!" she shrieked, breathing hard. "Don't snoop around, Heidi. Don't do it. Don't try to learn about my father. You'll regret it! I'm warning you!"

We both gasped as we looked down at her hand.

"Oh, noooo," she moaned.

She had squeezed the hamster to death.

12

I have to get away from this house, I decided.

I'd left Marianna sobbing in her room. She refused to listen to my apologies. And slammed her bedroom door in my face as I backed out of the room.

I can't believe she killed her hamster, I thought, shuddering. I can't believe she squeezed it like that.

Now she hates me, I realized. She blames me. Blames me . . .

She didn't like me before. But now she hates me.

Now she'll never tell me what she knows about her dad.

Now she'll never tell me what they were arguing about this morning. About the lies and secrets . . .

I felt so upset. My chest fluttered. My stomach felt hard as a rock.

"I have to go. . . . I have to go," I chanted to myself as I returned to my room.

I pulled on my parka and looked for my gloves. I pulled out all my dresser drawers and got down on my hands and knees to search the floor of the closet. But I couldn't find them anywhere.

"Forget the gloves," I muttered. "So you'll have cold hands. Get out, Heidi. Get out of the house."

I hurried outside. I had to get away from Marianna and her father. And their creepy, dark mansion. And all of their secrets.

The cold, fresh air made my cheeks tingle. The bright sun, high in a clear blue sky, felt warm on my skin.

I tossed back the parka hood and shook out my long brown hair. The hard snow crunched under my boots as I made my way along the walk that led to the side of the house.

From here, I could see the narrow road twisting down the hill to town. Only a few patches of snow here and there.

I found an old girls' bike in the garage. It probably belonged to Marianna.

I leaned heavily on the handlebars and tested the tires. They seemed full enough to carry me.

"Yes!" I cried happily. "Escape!"

A few seconds later, I was riding down the hill, pedaling hard, the tires bumping over the unpaved road, my hair flying behind me like a flag.

It felt so good. I wanted to sing and shout.

Above me, I saw Canada geese soaring high in a tight V formation. They honked noisily as they flew past.

Snow-covered pines became a green-and-white blur as I whirred downhill.

I stood up and pedaled, enjoying the exercise, the cool, sweet air, the feeling of freedom.

My good mood lasted until I reached the outskirts of the village.

Then I found myself back in the middle of a horror movie.

I slowed my bike as the first house came into view. I gazed at the metal shed behind the house. It lay on its side, one wall smashed in.

"Whoa," I murmured. The log fence around the backyard had a big gap in it. It looked as if it had been ripped apart. Logs were strewn over the snow, broken and bent.

The downstairs windows of the next house were shattered. Shards of glass were scattered over the snow, reflecting the morning sun. A side door had been ripped off its hinges. It tilted against the wall of the house.

It looks as if a tornado swept through here, I thought.

I pedaled on. I saw a group of men and women standing outside the house on the corner. They huddled around a car in the driveway, talking quietly, shaking their heads.

As I rode nearer, I saw that the car windshield had been smashed. A million cracks stretched out in the glass like spiderwebs.

The driver's door lay on the driveway beside the car, bent and battered. The steering wheel, wires dangling, poked out from beneath the car.

"What happened?" I called from the street.

The men and women turned to me. "Don't you know?" a woman called.

"Are you new here?" a man asked. "Haven't you heard?"

"Did you crawl out from under a rock?"

They seemed so angry, so unfriendly, I turned the corner and rode on.

"Be careful!" a man called after me. "Don't ride that thing at night!"

The bike tires crunched over broken glass. Two more cars had their windshields shattered.

A black-and-white police car was parked beside a small brick house on the next block. Two grim-faced officers were helping an old man reattach his front door.

All of the windows in the house were covered with newspaper. Broken glass littered the front yard.

A few seconds later, I turned another corner and found myself on the main street of town. A small crowd had gathered around a red-and-white truck, parked in the middle of the street.

I pedaled closer, then jumped off my bike. I read the bold letters on the side of the truck: ACTION NEWS 8.

Walking my bike up to the crowd, I saw a man with a video camera on his shoulder. In the center of the crowd, a young red-haired woman held a microphone.

A TV news crew, I realized. What *happened* here last night?

I pushed through the circle of people. The reporter poked the microphone into a familiar face.

Aaron!

He was talking to the woman, his eyes on the microphone. He didn't see me.

I moved close enough to hear what they were saying.

"And so the beast attacked again last night?" the reporter asked him.

Aaron gazed at the microphone. "Yes. It came running down the hill a little before eleven. And it started tearing things up."

"Were you outside that late? Did you see it come down the hill?" the reporter asked, turning her head and glancing at the snow-covered hill rising over the village.

"Well . . . no," Aaron replied. "I was home. My parents won't let me go out. My curfew is nine o'clock — because of the beast."

61

"Have you ever seen this creature?" the woman asked.

A truck rumbled by.

"Cut! Wait for the truck! It's too noisy!" the guy with the camera instructed.

They waited for the truck to pass. Then the camera guy signaled for Aaron to talk again.

"What was the question?" he asked.

"Have you ever seen the creature?" the woman repeated. She pushed the microphone up to Aaron's mouth.

"Yes."

"Is it human?"

"Well . . ." Aaron thought hard. "Sort of. It's about the size of a human. And it walks on two legs. Except it kind of staggers. But it's very furry."

"Furry?" the reporter asked.

Aaron nodded. "It has gray fur all over. On its arms. And its back. And it growls like a wolf or something."

"So it's an animal?" the woman asked.

Aaron rubbed his chin. "I'd say it's half-human, half-animal. I'd say —"

"Go up on the hill," a woman in the crowd shouted at the reporter. She stepped in front of Aaron and grabbed the microphone. "You want to get your news story? Don't waste your time down here. Go up to the big house up there. Dr. Jekyll's house. You want to see the monster? You'll find him in there!"

"*No, you won't!*" I cried. "I live in that house — and there's no monster in there!"

I gasped and clapped my hand over my mouth.

Why did I say that?

Why did I suddenly try to defend Uncle Jekyll?

Why didn't I keep my big mouth shut?

With cries of surprise, everyone turned to stare at me.

"Who is she?" someone asked.

"I've never seen her before," a young man replied.

Aaron narrowed his eyes at me. "Heidi? What are you doing here?" he whispered.

The others stared at me coldly, suspiciously.

I'm in trouble now, I realized.

I'm in major trouble.

"She's a Jekyll? *Get* her!" an angry voice growled.

gasped and took a step back.

Were they going to attack me?

No. No one moved. They circled me, staring at me so coldly — as if *I* were the beast!

"My uncle isn't a monster!" I cried, my voice trembling. "And there's no monster living in his house."

Did I really believe that?

I didn't know what to believe. But these people didn't know the truth, either.

Why should they accuse Uncle Jekyll when they had no proof?

I took another step back and tripped over my bike. I'd forgotten I'd set it down on the pavement. My heel caught the front wheel, and I fell hard, landing in a sitting position on top of it.

The young woman reporter hurried over and

reached out her free hand to help me up. Then she poked the microphone into my face. "Can you take us inside?" she asked eagerly.

I gaped at her. "Excuse me?"

"Can you take us inside your uncle's house? Can you let us see for ourselves?" she demanded.

"Uh . . . well . . ." I hesitated.

"See? She's lying!" a man shouted.

"She's a Jekyll. She's hiding the beast!" a woman cried.

"No . . . my uncle . . ." I stammered. "You have to get my uncle's permission," I told the reporter.

Then I turned to the crowd, my heart pounding, my throat so dry I could barely swallow. "I'm new here!" I cried. "I just moved here! I . . . I don't know anything!"

No one moved. No one spoke.

They stared so hard at me, as if trying to see inside my head.

They hate me, I thought. They don't even know me, and they hate me.

And then Aaron stepped forward, moving quickly.

His sudden movement startled me. I shrank back, thinking he planned to hurt me.

But he bent down and picked up my bike for me. "Heidi, you'd better go," he whispered. "Everyone in town is really upset. And scared."

"But, I —" I started.

"Last night was so terrifying," Aaron whispered. "No one knows what to do." He handed the bike to me. "Hurry. Go back to your uncle's house. You'll be safe there."

Will I? I wondered.

I jumped on the bike and started pedaling away. *Will* I be safe there?

I spent a dreary afternoon in the house. Uncle Jekyll never came out of his lab. I searched for Marianna but couldn't find her.

A freezing rain pounded the windows. The house was cold and damp. I pulled a heavy wool sweater over two T-shirts, but I still felt chilled.

I explored the house for a while, pulling open doors, searching rooms cluttered with old books and magazines.

I poked my head into the room with the scratched walls. I imagined a wild, snarling creature locked in there. I pictured it roaring furiously at it scraped long, curling claws over the walls. Shredding the wallpaper . . . shredding it . . . shredding it.

With a shudder, I backed out of the frightening room and pulled the door shut. I reminded myself not to go back there.

I made myself a sandwich for lunch. Then spent most of the afternoon reading in my room.

A few hours before dinner, a man arrived from the county phone company. Sylvia showed him into my room. I watched happily as he installed a phone on my desk.

"Yessss!" I cried after he left, pumping my fist in the air. I couldn't wait to try my new phone. I was desperate to call my friend Patsy back in Springfield.

"Well, Heidi? How is it?" she demanded after we said hi and how much we missed each other. "How is your new home?"

"Well..." I hesitated. I didn't want to tell her how strange and frightening everything was. But I couldn't hold it back. I had to tell someone.

"Patsy — it's awful here!" I cried, checking to make sure my bedroom door was closed. "My uncle Jekyll — he's totally weird. My cousin Marianna is so unfriendly. And there's a creature — some kind of creature that keeps attacking the village. The people here —"

I stopped, breathing hard.

And listened.

What was that clicking sound I kept hearing?

And then I heard breathing.

Not Patsy's breathing.

He's listening in! I realized.

Uncle Jekyll! He's listening on another phone! He's *spying* on me!

"What's that about a creature?" Patsy demanded. "You're kidding — right?"

"H-hold on a minute," I stammered.

I tossed the phone onto my bed and ran out of the room. I flew down the stairs and into the front hall.

Where was Uncle Jekyll? Where?

I wanted to catch him in the act. I wanted to know for sure if he was spying on me.

I spotted him on an armchair in the den. Sitting next to the phone.

As I burst into the room, I saw him pick up a book and pretend to read it. "Heidi? Hi." He pretended to be surprised to see me.

I stared at him, breathing hard, my mouth open.

I'm not safe here, I realized.

I'm trapped. I'm a prisoner here.

A strange smile spread over Uncle Jekyll's face. "Are you enjoying your new phone?" he asked.

15

The next night, I had a frightening dream. I knew I was dreaming, and I struggled to wake up. But I couldn't escape it.

A creature chased me across a snow-covered field. Growling, raging at the top of its lungs, it staggered after me on its hind legs.

Half-wolf, half-man, it raised its hairy snout to the sky and bellowed. Its red eyes glowed like fire, and thick gobs of yellow saliva ran down its furry chin.

I ran harder, harder. I leaned into a blowing wind and churned my legs, running so hard every muscle ached.

But my shoes slipped on the snowy surface. It was like running on a treadmill. I ran and ran but didn't move forward.

The beast roared closer. I saw it snap its jagged-toothed jaws. I felt its hot, sour breath on my hair and the back of my neck.

I tried to run harder. Harder. But I wasn't going anywhere. My shoes slid over the slick snow.

And then I fell. Facedown.

The creature leaped on top of me.

Its red eyes flamed above me. The thick yellow saliva puddled on my face, steaming hot.

"Nooooooo!" I wailed. I tried frantically to twist away. But it pinned me to the snow. So heavy . . . so heavy I couldn't breathe.

And then the creature opened its jaws. Lowered its head.

And sank its teeth into my shoulder.

I woke up with a sharp gasp.

The beast vanished. The white snow faded to black.

At first, I didn't know where I was. It took a few seconds to remember.

In a strange bed. In a strange room.

I sat up dizzily and rubbed my shoulder. It ached. It felt so sore.

From the dream?

My nightshirt was drenched with sweat. I climbed out of bed and, still shaky, made my way to the dresser. I clicked on the light. Found a clean nightshirt. And changed.

I glanced at the clock. Nearly four in the morning. Dark outside. And silent.

Images of the dream floated back to me. The chase. The horrifying roars of the creature. The hot breath on my neck.

I'll never get back to sleep, I realized. Maybe if I read for a while, I'll get sleepy again.

I took a few deep breaths. "Get over it, Heidi," I told myself out loud. "It was just a dream."

I made my way to the wall of books. Uncle Jekyll's old books. There must be something here to read, I thought. Maybe I can find something really boring that will put me right to sleep.

On a high shelf, I thought I spotted a children's book I'd loved as a kid. I reached for it. But my bare foot snagged on the edge of the carpet.

I stumbled forward. My shoulder bumped the bookshelf.

"Huh?" As I caught my balance, a board on the side of the shelf dropped down.

I moved over to it. A secret compartment.

I'd bumped open a secret compartment in the bookshelf.

I brought my face close and peered inside.

"Wow," I murmured. "What's hidden in there?"

16

I reached a hand in and pulled out an object. A book.

It appeared to be very old. It had a brown leather cover. The leather was cracked and crinkly.

I ran a finger over the faded letters on the front: DIARY.

An old diary.

I flipped through the pages. They were yellow and brittle. And covered with words, diary entries written in black ink in a tiny handwriting.

"Weird," I murmured. "Who would hide their diary inside a bookshelf?"

I carried the diary to the chair across from my bed and clicked on the floor lamp. Then, yawning, I settled into the chair and began to examine it.

I searched for the owner's name on the inside covers and on the first page. But the covers were blank except for yellow-brown age stains. And the first page began with the diary entry for January 1.

What year? What year?

The book didn't say. No owner. No date.

I blew dust off the spine. No information there.

I flipped through the pages again, careful not to tear the brittle paper. Then I opened the book somewhere near the beginning. Squinting at the tiny handwriting, I started to read:

... So cold today. The snow coming down in sheets, driven by the howling winds. I know I will howl too. I cannot control it. And I will go out in the storm. Because the storm inside me is more powerful than any snowstorm ...

"Huh?" I stared at the yellowed page, gripping the little book tightly in my lap.

What was this person writing about? A *storm* inside him?

Was that some kind of poetry?

I turned a few more pages and began reading again:

... I know what I did tonight. I remember every scream, every cry of horror. Those poor people. They don't deserve it. They don't deserve *me*.

But I am powerless to control it. At night when the urge comes over me, when my body makes its hideous changes . . . I must go out. What choice do I have?

I must run and rage and howl. And I must *feed*.

I know what I am on those terrifying but exciting nights. I am like a wild beast. And I live for the screams. And for the fear I create . . .

"Whoa!" I murmured. My heart pounded in my chest.

Wind rattled the windowpanes. I pulled the quilt from the bed over my chair and snuggled under it.

I started to read another page:

. . . Of course I am a human most of the time. A caring, frightened human. A human prisoner in this old house. And a prisoner in this body that changes at night. A prisoner in this body I cannot control.

Where does the rage come from? From where does the anger spring — the anger that forces me to kill and destroy? There are two of us trapped here. Two prisoners . . . the beast and the doctor . . .

The doctor?

I stared at the tiny handwriting, reading those words again and again until they blurred in front of my eyes.

The beast and the doctor . . .

74

Trapped in one body?

I shut the diary and studied the worn leather cover. Was I holding the diary of the *original* Dr. Jekyll?

Dr. Jekyll, who drank the potion and became the hideous, twisted, dangerous Mr. Hyde?

But how can that be? I asked myself, gripping the little book tightly.

Dr. Jekyll wasn't real — was he?

And then other questions flooded my mind. . . .

Did my uncle find this diary? Did Uncle Jekyll hide the diary in the secret compartment?

Did Uncle Jekyll study the old diary? Did he learn the original Dr. Jekyll's horrible secrets?

Has my uncle turned himself into a monster?

So many questions!

I didn't have time to think about answers.

I heard footsteps in the hall — and then my bedroom door swung open.

I tried to shove the diary under the quilt. "Uncle Jekyll?" I gasped.

No. No one there.

I realized the breeze from the hallway had swung the door open. I let out a long sigh of relief.

Shoving the quilt away, I climbed unsteadily to my feet. I flipped quickly through the diary, searching for the secret formula. No. No sign of it.

I carried the diary to the bookshelf and placed it carefully in its hiding place.

Then I closed the secret compartment, turned off the lights, and climbed into bed. I shut my eyes, but the tiny handwriting, the frightening words, still danced in front of my eyes.

The beast and the doctor . . .

Did Uncle Jekyll find the formula for the original Dr. Jekyll's potion? Was it hidden somewhere in the diary? Did he follow the directions and mix it himself?

And drink it?

Was my uncle the beast that was terrifying Shepherd Falls?

I couldn't stay here if he was.

I was in terrible danger.

I had to learn the truth — fast.

But how?

Lying in bed, tossing from side to side, wide awake, I thought of a plan.

I waited until after dinner the next night. Then I hid in Uncle Jekyll's lab.

I found the lab door closed. I turned the knob, pulled the door open, and crept inside.

The equipment churned and bubbled. On the long lab table, I saw two glass beakers half-filled with a purple liquid. A clear liquid dripped from a glass tube into a gallon-sized bottle.

Uncle Jekyll and Marianna were still at the dinner table. We'd had a quiet — almost silent — dinner. Marianna kept casting angry glances at her father. Uncle Jekyll pretended to ignore them.

"Are you going out tonight?" he asked her.

An odd question. I'd never seen Marianna leave the house.

"I don't know what I'm doing," she mumbled into her tuna casserole.

I asked to be excused, saying I didn't want any dessert.

I knew I had very little time to hide. My uncle always headed straight for his lab after dinner.

My eyes searched the long, cluttered room. Where could I hide? Where could I hide safely but still be able to spy on Uncle Jekyll?

A row of dark metal supply closets across from the lab table caught my eye. They looked like the hall lockers at my old school.

I darted over to them and began pulling open the doors one at a time. The narrow closets were all jammed with equipment. No room for me.

I heard Uncle Jekyll's voice out in the hall. He was arguing again with Marianna.

I searched desperately for a hiding place.

I'm going to be caught! I realized. He'll ask me what I'm doing in here. And I won't have an answer.

My heart thudding in my chest, I pulled open the last closet door. Yes! Only a few towels on the bottom.

I took a deep breath and squeezed inside. I pulled the metal door nearly closed — just as Uncle Jekyll stepped into the lab.

Peering through the narrow opening, I held my breath. Did he see me swing the door shut? Could he hear my heart pounding like a bass drum?

He moved to the table and inspected the beakers with the purple liquid.

He didn't see me, I realized. I slumped against the back of the closet and slowly let my breath out.

He poured the purple liquid carefully into a rack of slender glass test tubes. Then he adjusted some dials on the electronic equipment at the end of the table.

What is he working on? I wondered.

He is working so fast, so urgently. He must be in his lab at least twenty hours a day.

Why is he working so hard? What is he trying to do?

I hope it is something *good*, I prayed. I hope his work has nothing to do with the creature that is wrecking the village.

Maybe he's trying to cure a disease, I told myself. Maybe he's very close. He has almost found the cure. And he is working day and night because he knows he almost has it.

Or maybe he is in a race with another doctor. Uncle Jekyll wants to cure the disease before the other doctor beats him to it.

I desperately wanted my uncle to be *good*. I didn't want him to be a mad scientist. An evil villain. A . . . creature.

Please . . . I prayed . . . Please don't drink your formula and turn into a growling beast. Please . . . let the people in the town be wrong about you.

I watched as his hands moved furiously over the table. Pouring clear liquids into purple liquids. Turning knobs and dials. Mixing chemicals from one test tube to another. Holding glass beakers over a flame until the liquid inside bubbled and steamed.

Electricity sizzled over the table. Uncle Jekyll kept shocking the dark liquid in a beaker with some sort of electric probe.

His head bent, his shoulders slumped under the white lab coat, he worked feverishly, without ever stopping for a second, without coming up for air.

I began to feel cramped in the narrow closet. My knees ached. My back ached. Pressed against the metal sides, my arms had fallen asleep.

This was a big mistake, I decided. I'm not going to see anything interesting at all. I should have trusted Uncle Jekyll. I shouldn't be hiding in here spying on him.

I watched him raise a test tube to the fluorescent light over the table. It contained a rust-colored liquid that glowed in the light.

He studied it for a moment, turning it between his fingers.

Then he tilted back his head. Lowered the test tube to his mouth.

And drank the liquid down.

Oh, no, I thought, feeling heavy dread knot my throat. I pressed a hand over my mouth to keep from crying out.

Uncle Jekyll licked his lips. Then he raised another test tube with a green liquid inside — and poured that down his throat too.

He swallowed noisily and licked his lips.

Then he braced himself. He flattened both hands on the tabletop and leaned forward. As if waiting for the liquids to do something to him.

I stared through the narrow opening. I couldn't breathe. I couldn't move.

Leaning hard against the tabletop, Uncle Jekyll shut his eyes. His mouth twisted. His knees started to collapse.

Grabbing the tabletop to keep himself standing, he opened his mouth in a shrill howl of pain.

His eyes bulged and rolled in his head.

His face turned bright red.

Another painful howl escaped his throat. An animal howl. A *wolf* howl.

He clamped his eyes shut. He pounded the table with both hands. He tore at his white hair until it stood up in wild tufts.

His whole face twisted in agony.

And then, with an ugly groan from deep in his belly, he spun away from the table. And staggered to the door. Staggered like an animal, moaning and growling.

And vanished from the lab.

My heart throbbed. My chest ached. I realized I'd been holding my breath the whole time. I let it out in a loud whoosh.

I pushed open the closet door with my shoulder. And half fell, half leaped out of the narrow closet.

"I don't *believe* it," I murmured. "He *is* the beast. Uncle Jekyll *is* the creature."

My head spun. I raised both hands to my cheeks. My skin was burning hot!

What can I do? I asked myself.

Who can I tell?

I've got to stop him. I've got to get help for him. But who can help?

I couldn't think clearly. I couldn't think of anything at all.

I kept seeing the tortured expression on Uncle Jekyll's face. And hearing the animal howls that burst from his throat.

I stared at the empty test tubes lying on their sides on the table. How could he drink that stuff? *How?*

I've got to get out of here, I decided.

I turned to the door — and screamed.

Uncle Jekyll stood inside the doorway.

He had returned to the lab!

He was breathing hard, grunting with each breath, staring at me. Staring angrily.

"Heidi," he growled. "I'm so sorry you saw."

19

He lumbered toward me, his eyes rolling wildly.

"Wh-what are you going to do?" I stammered. I backed away from him, backed up until I hit the metal closets.

He grunted in reply. And grabbed my arm with both hands.

"Uncle Jekyll — stop!" I cried. "What are you doing?"

"Sorry you saw," he rasped again. His chest heaved up and down. His breath came in hoarse wheezes.

"Let go!" I pleaded.

But his grip tightened, and he pulled me away from the closets. I tried to pull back, but he was too strong.

He dragged me from the lab. Up the stairs. And pushed me into my room.

I spun around to face him. "Why are you doing this?" I cried.

He lurched into the hall and slammed the bedroom door shut. I heard the lock click.

I dove to the door. "Uncle Jekyll — I can help you! Let me help you! Don't lock me in here. Why are you doing this?"

"For your own good," he replied in a hoarse animal growl.

I heard his heavy footsteps going down the stairs.

I tried the door. Locked. He locked me in.

"Uncle Jekyll —" I called.

I knew he couldn't hear me. I heard the front door slam.

I ran to the bedroom window and peered out into the darkness.

After a few seconds, he staggered into view. I took a deep breath and tried to slow my racing heart as I watched him make his way down the hill toward the village. After a minute or so, he disappeared into the shadows.

"Why?" I murmured, shaking my head. "Why?"

Does he plan to keep me locked up in here forever? I asked myself.

No. He can't.

And then I thought of an even more frightening

question: What does he plan to do with me when he gets back?

Through the open window, I heard a shrill scream. And then frightened shouts from down the hill.

"I have to get out of here," I told myself.

I tried tugging the doorknob with all my strength. Then I tried to batter the door open with my shoulder.

No way. The door was solid oak.

I dove to the window. I heard more screams from town. Flames shot up. More angry cries. A siren wailed.

I leaned out the window and looked down. A two-story drop straight to the ground. No tree to climb down. No shrubs below to break my fall.

"I can't jump out," I decided. "I'll break my neck."

Then I spotted the metal rain gutter at the corner of the house. Rusted, its paint peeling, it ran along the roof, then straight down nearly to the ground.

If I can wrap my hands around it, I can slide down, I decided. But will it hold my weight?

Only one way to find out.

I leaned farther out the window and reached for it . . . reached . . .

No. It was inches from my grasp. I couldn't lean any farther. I couldn't reach it.

Wait, I thought. I ducked back into the room and pulled the desk chair to the window. My legs trembling, I climbed onto the desk chair. Then I leaned out the window again.

Reached . . . reached for the gutter.

My fingers brushed the rusted metal —

— and then I lost my balance.

I felt my body plunging forward . . . plunging out the window . . .

. . . and I fell.

20

I screamed — and grabbed wildly for the gutter.

My hands wrapped around it. The rusted metal scraped my skin.

I cried out and held on. Sliding . . . sliding too fast.

The pain grew too intense.

My hands flew off the gutter.

I landed hard on my back.

I didn't feel the landing. I didn't feel anything.

My wind was knocked out. I gasped for breath.

I'm dying, I thought.

But then I pulled in a wheezing breath. And, ignoring the pain, forced it out.

Above me, the house came back into view. And above it, the sky, pink with a high blanket of gray clouds.

I sucked in another breath. Another. The air felt so cool.

I began to feel again. Felt the snow on the back of my neck. Felt the cold dampness of the ground through my clothes.

My hands throbbed and burned, burned from sliding on the rusted metal gutter.

I sat up.

And heard a scream. And sirens down the hill.

"Uncle Jekyll —" I choked out.

I climbed unsteadily to my feet. The ground rocked and bobbed beneath me. I shut my eyes, waiting for my legs to stop trembling.

"I'm okay," I murmured. I bent down and rubbed cold snow on my burning hands.

Then I began jogging down the hill.

What did I plan to do when I reached the village?

I didn't know. I couldn't think clearly. But I had nowhere else to run.

Maybe I can save Uncle Jekyll, I thought.

A deafening explosion made me stop. Somewhere in the village a mountain of flames burst up like a volcano erupting.

Shrill screams and cries rose up over the roar of the flames. In the flickering yellow-orange light, I could see people running frantically in all directions.

Maybe I can pull Uncle Jekyll away from there, I thought.

I instantly realized it was a crazy idea.

He was a *beast* now, an inhuman creature.

He had to be stopped.

Breathing hard, I reached the edge of the village. I heard the crack of gunshots. I ran past an overturned car, its tires spinning.

I turned onto the main street. Police officers patrolled, guns out, ready for action. In the orange light of the fires, their faces were grim and angry.

"Get away from here!" a man shouted.

It took me a few seconds to realize he was shouting at me.

"Stay out of town!"

"The beast is angry tonight!"

"Get off the street!"

Their shouts rang out over the crackling of the fires, the wail of sirens, the terrified screams. They hurried away, toward a burning house on the next block.

I turned, eager to get off the street.

Too late.

"Noooooo!" I uttered a shocked scream as the creature leaped out from the side of a house.

A wolf! A snarling wolf-creature, howling, snapping his wet jaws. His gray-and-brown fur bristling. Lumbering forward stiffly on two legs.

His red eyes glowed and then locked on me.

I backed across a snow-covered lawn. Too late to run.

Too late to hide.

The growling creature moved quickly, arching his body for the attack.

I searched frantically for a weapon. A stick. A tree branch. Something to use to bat it away.

No. Nothing.

With a hideous roar, the beast spread his furry arms — and dove at me.

21

With a terrified cry, I dropped to the ground. My face plunged into the hard-packed snow.

I jerked my head up in time to see the beast sail over me.

I tried to scramble away.

But before I could climb to my feet, I felt a heavy paw on my back.

"No!" I gasped.

Grunting loudly, the beast pushed me down. Held me down on the snow.

"Uncle Jekyll —" I choked out. "Please . . ."

I turned and saw him tilt up his head and send an animal roar to the sky.

And then I saw a figure come running across the street.

Aaron!

Yes. Aaron. Waving a baseball bat in front of him with both hands.

"Heidi — run!" he cried breathlessly. Flames from a burning car lit up his face, and I could see the fear on his twisted features. "Run!"

"I . . . can't!" I gasped. "The beast — he has me pinned down."

Aaron came running, swinging the bat furiously.

The beast let go of me. Roaring angrily, he rose onto his hind legs and spun around to face Aaron.

"It's my uncle!" I cried to Aaron. "The beast is my uncle! I saw him drink a chemical and —"

Another angry roar drowned out my words.

"Run!" Aaron cried shrilly, his dark eyes reflecting the firelight. "The people — the people of the village are going to destroy him! We can't take it anymore! They plan to go up the hill, Heidi. They plan to burn down your uncle's house!"

"No!" I gasped.

And then my cry was cut short as the beast shoved me roughly aside.

Aaron swung the baseball bat.

The beast grabbed it from Aaron's hands — and flung it across the snow.

I screamed again as the snarling creature dove at Aaron.

The beast picked Aaron up easily in both hairy paws. Lifted him high in the air.

And threw him into the fire.

22

My entire body locked in horror as I watched Aaron disappear into the flames.

I forced myself to move. Forced myself to run to the fire to help him.

But the beast blocked my path. Clawed at me. Swung a huge, powerful arm. His sharp claws sliced through my jacket.

He swiped again, aiming for my face.

I dove to the ground, sprawling onto my elbows and knees.

Climbing up, I saw Aaron come scrambling out of the fire. He rolled in the snow. Rolled over and over.

And then jumped to his feet. "I'm okay, Heidi!" he called to me, cupping his hands around his mouth. "Run!"

I gazed at him for a moment, making sure he wasn't burned. Making sure he really was okay.

The snarling beast lurched at me again.

The creature dove with such fury, he lost his balance. He slipped to his knees in the snow.

And I took off.

I ran past the burning car, past houses with their windows shattered, past a speeding patrol car, its siren blaring. Then I headed up the hill.

Why was I returning to the house?

I had nowhere else to run.

Halfway up the hill, I turned back.

And to my horror, I saw the snarling beast following me.

"Ohhhhh." A terrified moan escaped my throat.

Now what? Now what?

I couldn't think.

I burst into the house, my chest heaving, my throat aching. The dark entryway spun before me.

Where to go? Where can I hide? Is there any place I will be safe?

I'll hide until the potion wears off, I decided. Yes! Maybe the potion will wear off. And then I can talk to Uncle Jekyll, try to reason with him.

Maybe . . . Maybe I can convince him to send me somewhere safe.

But where?

This is my home now.

My home . . .

But not for long. The villagers will soon be coming to burn it down!

And then what?

Too many thoughts. I squeezed my hands against my head. My brain felt ready to explode!

I heard a low growl from outside. In my terror, I had left the front door wide open!

He'll be in here any second. I've got to hide — now! I decided.

I spun away from the door and went running through the hall. The door to my uncle's lab stood open, all the lights on.

I burst inside, panting, my side aching.

I glanced around frantically, searching for a hiding place.

Should I go back into the closet? Would he find me there?

My eyes stopped at the lab table — and another crazy idea flashed into my head.

Drink the potion, Heidi, I told myself.

Drink the same potion your uncle drank — and become a beast too. If you don't, you won't stand a chance. It's the only way you can fight him.

Was it a crazy idea? Or a brilliant idea?

I didn't have time to decide. I heard the beast's heavy footsteps in the hall.

I lurched to the table. Grabbed the test tube. And raised it to my lips.

23

Empty.

The test tube was empty.

I shook it. I peered into it.

Of *course* it was empty. I had watched Uncle Jekyll drink it down.

I grabbed up the one beside it. He had drunk from both of them. The second one was empty too.

It fell from my hand as the beast swept into the lab. His fur-covered feet thudded wetly over the floor. He pulled his dark lips back, baring jagged wolf teeth.

"Uncle Jekyll —" I choked out, backing away.

His red eyes locked on mine. Teeth still bared, he uttered a low animal grunt.

And stepped toward me.

"Uncle Jekyll — it's me — Heidi," I called in a

shrill, quivering voice. "Do you recognize me? Do you know me?"

The beast grunted again in reply.

"You wouldn't hurt me, would you?" I cried. "Please. You wouldn't hurt your own niece — would you?"

He opened his jaws in an angry roar and swiped a paw angrily in front of him.

Waving his arm in front of him, as if clearing a path, he moved toward me, snarling, grunting, wheezing.

I backed up against the wall.

Trapped. Nowhere to run.

He moved in slowly, steadily. Growling sharply now. Snapping his jaws. A white froth bubbled over his lips.

I raised my hands in front of me, trying to shield myself.

The beast raised both arms to attack.

And then I heard a sound behind him. A sound from the lab door.

The beast stopped — and turned away from me.

I gaped over his furry shoulder — and saw a figure hurry into the lab.

Uncle Jekyll!

"Heidi —" Uncle Jekyll cried from the doorway. "Are you okay?"

I opened my mouth to reply — but no sound came out.

Uncle Jekyll?

Trembling all over, I gazed from the growling beast to Uncle Jekyll.

I was wrong! I realized to my shock.

Uncle Jekyll *isn't* the beast!

The creature raked a paw at Uncle Jekyll, as if warning him away. Then it turned to me, opened its jaws in an angry roar, and arched its back, preparing to pounce.

Uncle Jekyll leaped across the room. He tackled the snarling creature from behind. Wrapped his arms around its waist and wrestled it . . . wrestled it away from me.

The beast struggled to free itself, thrashing its furry arms, bending its knees, heaving its shoulders.

But Uncle Jekyll held on tight. Hugging the angry creature . . . hugging it . . . hugging it . . .

Until the beast surrendered. Stopped its struggles.

With a long sigh, the creature lowered its head and shut its eyes. Its shoulders slumped. Its whole body sagged.

And still Uncle Jekyll held on, hugging it, hugging it so tightly, I wondered if it could breathe.

And as my uncle hugged it, pressing his head against the furry back, the creature began to change.

To shrink . . .

The fur pulled back into the skin.

The light faded from the blazing red eyes. The frothing snout melted into the face.

As I stared in silent shock, the beast shrunk . . . hunched in on itself . . .

And when it raised its head, it had turned back into — Marianna!

Her black curls fell wetly, covering her face. Her shoulders heaved up and down. She pressed her face against her father's chest. And cried softly.

Uncle Jekyll held her tightly. And raised his sad, red-rimmed eyes to me. "Heidi, I locked you in your room to keep you safe," he said, his voice just above a whisper. "I warned you to stay there. I didn't want you to get involved."

"I . . . I tried to help," I stammered, still staring in shock at Marianna. Marianna the Beast. "Uncle Jekyll, I didn't know. . . ." The words caught in my throat.

Marianna raised her head. Tears rolled down her swollen cheeks. "Daddy," she whispered. "What am I going to do?"

Uncle Jekyll patted her hair gently. "I don't know, Marianna," he replied. "I spend all my time trying to find a cure for you. You know I'm here in the lab, working on it night and day."

A sob escaped Marianna's throat. "I can't go on like this, Dad. Being a person in the daytime . . . and a creature at night."

"I know, I know," Uncle Jekyll said softly. "Some day soon, I will find the right cure. If I just keep trying. I drink it myself. I test each one on myself to see what it does. You know that I'll do anything to find the right mixture to keep you from transforming."

I swallowed hard. "Uncle Jekyll, how did this happen?" I asked quietly. "Why does this happen to Marianna?"

He uttered a sigh. "It happened five years ago. Marianna was seven. We were traveling in Europe. Our car broke down in the middle of a forest."

He sighed again. "I remember it so clearly," he

said, still hugging Marianna. "She got bored while the car was being fixed. She wandered into the forest and got lost. When I finally found her . . ."

He swallowed a sob. "When I finally found Marianna, she told me about a forest creature. It attacked her. It bit her. I didn't know whether to believe her or not. She was always making up stories."

He gently patted Marianna's hair. "One bite of the creature was all it took to ruin Marianna's life. A few weeks later, Marianna transformed for the first time. And now, most nights, she transforms into a frightening, angry beast. I . . . I've been searching for a cure ever since. I think I'm close, but —"

He stopped.

Marianna raised her head, suddenly alert.

All three of us heard the angry shouts. The thud of boots on the hill.

"No!" Uncle Jekyll let out a scream as a rock came crashing through the lab window.

And then we heard the steady chant from the villagers outside: "Kill the beast . . . kill the beast . . . kill the beast!"

25

"**K**ill the beast ... kill the beast ..."

The sound of the ugly chant burst through the shattered window.

"Burn it down!" someone shouted. "Burn the house down!"

We heard people battering the front door. And more wild, angry shouts:

"Burn the house!"

"First, kill the beast!"

"Kill the evil!"

Another rock sailed into the lab. It hit a shelf of beakers on the wall. Shattered glass flew across the room.

Uncle Jekyll's eyes bulged wide in fear. He still had his arms around Marianna. But she pulled away in panic, lurched toward the lab door, then turned back. "Dad — what do we do?"

Uncle Jekyll uttered a long, sad sigh. He stared at the broken window.

"Kill the beast . . . kill the beast . . ." The angry chants grew louder. The pounding on the front door sounded like booms of thunder.

"Are we trapped in here?" I cried, shouting over the wild cries and chanting voices. "They're out of control. They'll kill us all!"

Uncle Jekyll grabbed my hand and pulled me toward Marianna at the door. "I planned for this," he said. "We can escape. But we have to be fast."

We ran into the hall. And heard a loud cracking sound.

"The front door!" I gasped. "They've broken it down."

"This way!" Uncle Jekyll cried.

He led us along the back hall. We turned a corner into a narrow hallway I'd never seen.

I heard angry cries. From inside the house! Heavy footsteps.

I smelled smoke. "They're setting the house on fire!" I cried.

Uncle Jekyll pulled open a narrow door. "In here," he instructed. He moved aside. Marianna and I stepped inside.

Uncle Jekyll pulled the door closed behind us. A steep stairway led down to the basement. Our shoes thudded on the creaking stairs as we made our way down.

"They'll search for us. They'll find us down here," Marianna whispered to her father. "If they burn the house, we'll be trapped."

Uncle Jekyll raised a finger to his lips. His eyes were narrowed in determination. Ducking his head under the low ceiling, he guided us through the cluttered basement. Past the enormous, chugging, vibrating furnace. Past a storage area piled high with wooden cartons and old steamer trunks.

He picked up a flashlight on a worktable and clicked it on. Then we followed the darting beam of light through two large, empty spaces, our footsteps echoing on the concrete floor. And stopped at a tall wooden crate against the far wall.

"Help me," Uncle Jekyll instructed. He leaned his shoulder against the crate and started to push. Marianna and I moved to the other side and pulled.

Above us, I heard heavy footsteps. Angry shouts. The villagers were searching the house.

The crate slid an inch at a time. Finally, we moved it far enough to reveal a low opening in the basement wall.

"It's a tunnel," Uncle Jekyll said, wiping sweat from his forehead with his coat sleeve. "An escape tunnel."

I peered into the low, dark opening. "Where does it lead?"

"It goes down the hill. Past the village," Uncle Jekyll replied. "It ends less than a mile from the highway. We'll be safe. And maybe we can get a ride to somewhere far away."

A loud crash upstairs made me jump. The sharp smell of smoke drifted down through the basement ceiling.

"Hurry," Uncle Jekyll urged. "We want to be out of the tunnel before they search the basement."

I ducked my head and stepped into the narrow opening. My eyes adjusted slowly to the darkness. Uncle Jekyll aimed the flashlight at our feet.

The tunnel was concrete, low and round, cut into the hill. I heard the scuttle of tiny feet up ahead. Field mice? Raccoons? Rats?

No time to worry about them.

Hunching low, we began making our way through the tunnel. It curved slowly and then began to slope down. The circle of light from the flashlight danced on the floor ahead of us.

No one spoke. The only sounds now were the scrape of our shoes on the tunnel floor and our rapid, shallow breathing.

I kept listening for footsteps behind us. But the villagers hadn't discovered the tunnel yet.

After a minute or two, I stopped.

"Whoa. Wait," I called. My voice echoed off the low walls.

"What's wrong?" Uncle Jekyll demanded. "We have a long way to go, Heidi."

"I know," I replied. "But I have to go back. I forgot something."

"No — you can't!" Marianna cried out, her voice trembling in fright. "They'll capture you. They'll *kill* you!"

"What did you forget?" Uncle Jekyll demanded. "It can't be important enough to —"

"It's a diary," I told him. "A very old diary."

"No, Heidi —" my uncle started.

But I didn't give him a chance to finish. I spun away from them and took off, back toward the basement.

I knew that going back up to the house was crazy. But the old diary was too valuable to leave behind. It was probably worth a fortune. And it was part of history.

I couldn't let it burn with the rest of the house. I couldn't let such an important document be lost forever.

I had to rescue it.

"Heidi   come back!" Uncle Jekyll's cry rang out through the tunnel, far behind me now.

I turned a corner, and the tunnel opening came into view. I hunched under the low ceiling and stepped into the basement.

Thick smoke choked my throat. I heard shouts upstairs. Running footsteps.

I took a deep breath and held it. Then, pressing my hand over my nose and mouth, I made my way to the basement stairs.

Could I get up to my room?

Could I rescue the old diary from its secret hiding place — and make my escape again?

I had to try.

louds of thick, sour smoke billowed around me. Holding my breath, my eyes stinging, I ran to the stairs.

I hesitated at the top of the stairs and listened. Were there villagers on the other side of the door?

My lungs were bursting. I couldn't stay there. I had to breathe.

I pushed open the basement door and stepped into the back hallway. Letting my breath out in a *whoosh*, I peered up and down the hall.

I heard angry shouts from the front of the house. The crackle of flames.

I pressed myself against the wall as a group of men in the next hallway thundered by. Holding my breath again, I waited until they ran out of sight. Then, keeping close to the wall, I began inching my way to the front stairway.

As I passed the kitchen, I saw two men with axes, furiously chopping away at the sink and counter.

"Destroy everything!" someone shouted.

"This is what he did to our town!" someone else cried.

"Where is he? Don't let him escape!"

"Did anyone search the roof?"

"Is there a basement?"

The drapes in the den were on fire. Flames leaped up from the couch.

In the living room a group of boys about my age were smashing the front window. Tearing apart the furniture.

I backed into a closet as two men ran past carrying flaming torches.

"Where is the beast?"

"He didn't go far!"

"He won't leave this house!"

Their angry words stabbed at me like knives.

You don't know the truth, I thought bitterly. You don't know that Marianna is the beast. That she can't help herself. You don't know how hard my uncle is working to find a cure. To rid the village of the beast.

But that didn't matter now. Uncle Jekyll and Marianna would never be able to return to the village. Never be able to return to their house.

The house will be destroyed before the villagers leave, I realized.

An explosion of bright flames lit up the hall.

I peered out from the closet. The coast was clear.

I lurched to the stairs, and leaning forward, I began running up them at full speed.

Please, please, let me get to my bedroom, I prayed.

Let me find the hidden diary. And let me return to the tunnel, return to Marianna and Uncle Jekyll.

Then I never want to see this village again.

I reached the top of the stairs, breathing hard. I could hear cries and shouts in Marianna's room at the end of the hall.

A loud crash made me gasp. They were destroying her room too.

I darted into my room. The room looked as if a tornado had swept through. My dresser drawers had been pulled out and tossed onto the floor. My clothes had been strewn everywhere.

The window curtains had been ripped off their rod. The window smashed. Glass everywhere.

I didn't care.

I dove for the bookshelf. Pulled down the board over the hidden compartment.

Was the old diary still inside?

Yes.

I grabbed it with a trembling hand. My hand shook so hard, I nearly dropped it.

Glancing over my shoulder to the door, I tucked the diary into my coat pocket.

111

I took one last glance at the room and then, with a shudder, made my way back to the hall.

I stopped when I heard excited voices in the next room.

"Is there an attic? There has to be an attic."

"If he's hiding up there, we'll find him."

I turned and began running to the stairs. I could feel the diary bouncing in my pocket.

I stopped at the top of the stairs. Peered down. No one there.

I reached for the banister.

And strong hands grabbed me from behind.

I turned to see two men, eyes wild, hair matted wetly to their heads, sweat running down their faces.

"I've got one!" one of them cried, gripping my shoulder tightly.

"Yes!" the other cheered. "We've got one!" He lowered his sweating face to me. "Lead us to the beast!" he snarled. "Lead us to the beast now — or your life is over!"

27

"N o —" I screamed. I struggled to squirm out of their grasp.

But they were too strong.

"Tell us where the beast is!" one of them growled, squeezing my arm. "Tell us now, and we'll let you go."

"But — I don't know!" I cried. "I just moved here. I . . . I really don't know what you're talking about!"

The two men narrowed their eyes at me, studying me suspiciously.

"She's lying," one of them snapped.

"Tell us the truth," his partner demanded, spitting the words in my face. "Tell us the truth or you'll never leave this house!"

"Let her go!" a voice called.

All three of us turned to see Aaron running down the hall.

"Let her go!" he told them again. "She doesn't know anything. I met her at the bus station on Monday. She just arrived here."

The two men ignored Aaron. One of them let go of my arm. But he didn't back away. "Have you seen the beast? Where is he hiding?" he shouted.

"Tell us!" his friend demanded again.

Flames crackled behind them. Angry shouts rang out through the house.

"I — I don't know," I stammered. "I really don't know."

Aaron grabbed my hand. "I'm taking her out of here. Can't you see she's telling the truth?" He pulled me away.

We started to run. Thick, sour smoke swirled through the hall. My eyes watering, I glanced back. The two men hadn't moved. They weren't following us.

"We've got to get out fast," Aaron cried. "They're going to destroy the whole house. They won't stop until they capture your uncle."

"This way." I tugged him through the back hall. Then down the basement stairs.

Our shoes thudded over the concrete floor. I led Aaron to the tunnel, and we burst inside it. Then, running hard, we followed it as it sloped down the hill.

I kept glancing back, praying that no one was following us.

We seemed to run for miles. I was breathing hard, my side aching, when we finally climbed out the other end.

"Uncle Jekyll? Marianna?" I called their names breathlessly.

No sign of them.

Did they escape to safety?

Did they get away?

Would I ever see them again?

So many frantic questions ran through my mind.

Pulling my wet hair off my forehead, I gazed around. The tunnel had led us past the village, to a row of low hills that faced the highway.

The village stood quiet and empty behind the low hills. I turned, struggling to catch my breath.

In the distance, high above the village, I could see a wall of orange-and-yellow flames, so bright, so bright against the purple night sky.

The flames appeared to reach up to the moon.

Uncle Jekyll's house. Burning . . . burning to the ground. The heat and smoke swept down the hill. Washed over Aaron and me.

My eyes welled with tears. The heat and smoke stung my face.

But I didn't move. I stared up at the house, watching it burn, watching it vanish in the raging flames . . . until Aaron gently pulled me away.

*　　*　　*

Later, we sat in Aaron's kitchen. His mother gave us dinner. She said I could stay with them until we contacted my other relatives.

Outside, we could hear the villagers returning from the hill. I knew they had to be unhappy. They destroyed Uncle Jekyll's house, but they didn't capture the beast.

I trembled, picturing the fire, the wall of flames reaching up to the sky. I wondered if Uncle Jekyll and Marianna were somewhere safe.

Yes. They had to be. By now, they were far away from here.

The horror was over. . . .

"Hey!" I suddenly remembered the diary.

"Aaron, I have to show you something," I said. I hurried to the closet, pulled the diary from my coat pocket, then returned to the kitchen.

Aaron stared at the little book. "What's that?"

"This is why I went back to the house," I told him excitedly. "It's an old diary. I found it hidden in my bedroom. I think it's very valuable. I think it's the diary of the original Dr. Jekyll."

"Huh?" Aaron's mouth dropped open. "Let me see that."

He took the diary from my hand and examined the worn, faded cover. Then he started to skim through it, squinting at the tiny handwriting.

"Whoa. Heidi?" He raised his eyes to me. "It's not an old diary. Check this out."

He handed it up to me, open to one of the first pages. I read it out loud:

"*This diary is the property of Marianna Jekyll.*"

I let out a gasp. "I didn't see this page," I told Aaron. "So it's Marianna's diary! Wow! She used a faded, old diary. But the entries were new."

When did she stop writing in it? I wondered. I flipped through the pages until I found the last entry in the book.

Then I brought the diary close to my face and started to read.

As I read Marianna's words, I froze, gripped in horror, gripped in the fear that *my* horror was only beginning:

. . . I hid the diary in my cousin Heidi's room. I never want anyone to find it. I never want anyone to know my shame, to know what I have done. I was out of control . . . that is my only excuse.

Soon after Heidi arrived, I was a creature. I was not myself. I crept into Heidi's room to write in my diary. I saw her sleeping there. I had no control. She slept so soundly . . . I leaned over her bed . . . I BIT her shoulder . . . bit her . . . bit her . . .

Trembling, I raised my eyes to find Aaron staring hard at me.

"Heidi — what's wrong?" he asked. "Why do you look so strange?"

About R.L. Stine

R.L. Stine is the most popular author in America. He is the creator of the *Goosebumps, Give Yourself Goosebumps, Fear Street,* and *Ghosts of Fear Street* series, among other popular books. He has written over 250 scary novels for kids. Bob lives in New York City with his wife, Jane, teenage son, Matt, and dog, Nadine.

Welcome to the new millennium of fear

Check out this
chilling preview of
what's next from
R.L. STINE

Scream School

Jake loved going over to Carlos's house. His parents had their own screening room with a movie projector and full-size screen. And they had the most amazing collection of old horror movies.

Carlos and Jake loved to watch the classic black-and-white films: *Bride of Frankenstein, The Wolfman, The Invisible Man.*

The two of them screamed their heads off, even though the old films seemed kind of funny now.

One day, Jake told his dad how much he enjoyed the old horror movies.

"Great old stuff," Emory replied. "If you ever get too scared while you're watching, just remind yourself that it's only a movie."

Jake dribbled the ball past Carlos. Carlos slapped at it and missed. Jake went up for his shot.

"Hey, Jake —" A voice from the driveway.

Jake turned. Missed the shot. The ball hit the rim and bounced away.

Chelsea came running over, her light-brown hair flying behind her. She wore a white tennis outfit and carried a tennis racket. "What are you guys doing?" she asked.

"Knitting a sweater," Jake replied. He was still angry that she had laughed at him at dinner the night before. "What does it look like we're doing?"

Chelsea pretended to hit him on the head with her tennis racket. "I meant, are you playing a game or just messing around?"

"Both," Carlos replied, grinning. "Want to play? How about Jake and me against you?"

"No way," Chelsea replied. She set her racket down on the grass beside the court. "Basketball isn't my sport. I kind of stink at it."

"Okay. You and Jake against me," Carlos suggested. "I'll try to go easy on you two."

They started their game. Chelsea tried to dribble the ball past Carlos, who danced in front of her, waving both hands in her face.

"Pass it! Pass it!" Jake cried.

Chelsea dribbled to the basket. Shot and scored.

"Lucky shot," Carlos murmured.

He took the ball out. Started to dribble, dancing to one side, then the other. Fancy footwork.

Showing off for Chelsea, Jake thought.

Chelsea moved in front of Carlos — and stole

the ball from his hands. She dribbled, backing over the half-court line, then moved forward.

"Pass it! Here!" Jake called, waving his arms over his head. "I'm open!"

Chelsea ignored him and fired off a two-handed layup. It swished through the basket. "Four to zip," she told Carlos.

"Hey — am I in this game or what?" Jake complained.

"Know what Jake did yesterday on his dad's movie set?" Chelsea asked Carlos. She cast a mischievous, teasing glance at Jake.

"No, what?" Carlos asked, dribbling in place.

"Shut up, Chelsea!" Jake snapped. "Just shut up!"

"What did he do?" Carlos asked, grinning at Chelsea.

Chelsea opened her mouth to reply.

But all three of them froze when they heard the loud growls. And saw the enormous black rottweiler come roaring into the yard.

The ball fell out of Carlos's hands and rolled away.

"Oh, no . . . I know this dog," Jake moaned, backing up.

Barking furiously, the huge dog lowered its head, preparing to attack.

"No, Dukie! No!" Jake pleaded. He raised both hands, trying to shield himself. "Dukie — down! Down!"

The dog opened its jaws in a furious growl.

"Oh . . . help!" Jake cried as the dog raised its front paws. Leaped heavily onto him. Knocked Jake to the ground.

And lowered its massive head to attack.

ukie — no! Nooooo!" Jake howled.

But the dog stood over Jake, its big paws pressing Jake's shoulders to the ground. It lowered its head. And licked.

Licked . . .

"Dukie — stop! Dukie!" Jake pleaded.

The dog licked Jake's face . . . licked his neck. Its stubby tail wagged furiously.

In seconds, Jake's cheeks and neck were glistening with wet dog slime.

"Pull him off!" Jake begged his friends. "He does this to me all the time. He thinks he's still a puppy. Owww! He weighs a *ton*! Owww! Dukie — you're *crushing* me!"

Chelsea and Carlos looked on helplessly.

Dukie finally got tired of giving Jake a tongue

bath. He backed off, panting, his tail twirling like a propeller.

Jake saw his father trotting across the lawn. "Emory?"

Dukie bounded over to greet Mr. Banyon. The dog's tongue trailed from its mouth as it ran.

Emory gave its head a few pats, then dropped beside Jake. "You okay?" he asked.

Jake pulled himself up to a sitting position. He wiped sticky dog saliva off his cheek with the back of one hand. "Yeah. Fine."

Emory's face filled with concern. He placed a hand on Jake's shoulder. "Jake — why didn't you ever tell me that you're scared of dogs?"

Jake squinted up at his father. "Huh?"

"I had no idea," Emory continued, shaking his head. "But don't worry. We can deal with the problem."

"Problem? What problem?" Jake cried.

Chelsea and Carlos watched from the basketball court. Carlos picked up the ball and tossed it from hand to hand.

"The first thing is to admit it," Emory told Jake. "Admit that you're afraid of dogs. Once you realize you have a problem, we can —"

"But I'm *not* — !" Jake protested. "Emory, I just —"

"I saw the whole thing, Jake," Emory replied, patting Jake's shoulder again.

"Dukie is pretty scary," Chelsea chimed in.

"He is *not!*" Jake cried angrily. "I've known him since he was a puppy. And he's just playful, that's all."

Emory climbed to his feet. He reached down and pulled Jake up. "Know what? I'll get you a dog, Jake. Your birthday is coming up. I'll buy you a dog for your birthday. That will help you work out your problems."

"But, Emory — if you'd only listen to me . . ."

"Having your own dog will help you get over your fear."

A phone rang. Emory pulled a cell phone from the pocket of his khakis. He flipped it open and began talking into it as he walked back to the house.

Jake turned to his friends. They both had wide grins on their faces.

"Look out, Jake — the neighbors' cat is over there," Carlos said, pointing.

"We'll protect you," Chelsea teased. "Don't be afraid. We won't let it get you."

Laughing scornfully, they slapped each other a high five.

Jake let out an angry, frustrated cry. He grabbed the basketball — and heaved it as high and as hard as he could.

All three of them watched it sail high into the sky, bounce once on the grass, and then splash into the swimming pool.

"Nice shot," Carlos murmured.

Jake just growled in reply.

That night, Jake stepped out of Carlos's house and began walking home. It was a clear, warm night. A million stars glittered overhead. The light from a full moon made the perfectly trimmed Beverly Hills lawns shimmer like silver.

Jake crossed the street onto the next block. The houses were mostly dark. Streetlamps cast yellow light, making his shadow stretch far in front of him.

A warm breeze brushed against him as he walked. The breeze rustled the low hedges along the sidewalk.

A screech in a tree limb made Jake gaze up. A bird? A cat?

He couldn't see.

To his surprise, the stars had all vanished. He watched a black cloud slide quickly over the moon.

The ground darkened. His shadow faded into the deepening blackness.

So dark now. Suddenly so dark.

Eerily dark.

He crossed the street and stepped into a thick, damp mist. A strange green glow against the darkness. Swirling snakes of green cloud, hovering low against the ground, curling around his ankles.

The thick green fog curling around him, washing over him. Sweeping so silently around him, as if pulling him inside.

Holding him in its green glow. Holding him . . . pressing against him so wetly . . . trapping him.

"Hey —" Jake uttered a strangled cry.

He took another step. His legs suddenly felt as heavy as lead.

"Hey —"

Only two blocks to go until he was home. Why couldn't he see the houses now? What happened to the light from the streetlamps?

He heard a rustling behind the hedge. Footsteps.

"Hey —"

Why couldn't he see the hedge?

The green fog wrapped around him, tightening its grip, so warm and wet.

He couldn't see. Couldn't see anything.

"Hey — hey — what's *happening*?"

ake heard scrambling behind the hedge. A frantic rustling like small animals scampering over leaves.

"I can't see anything," he murmured.

And then the thick green mist appeared to split apart.

And a figure loomed quickly in front of him. A figure of shimmering blue shadows. So tall and thin . . . taller than a human.

And then from out of the shadows, a face. A haunted, distorted face.

And Jake cried out in shock — "Johnny Scream!"

Johnny's silver eyes glared down at Jake, glowing green, reflecting the mist. His black lips curled in a cold smile. He stretched out bony arms as if trying to block Jake's way.

"Wh-what are you doing here?" Jake stammered.

"I was walking home, and this weird fog came up, and —"

"You can't go home," Johnny Scream rasped. The curled fingernails clicked on his clenching fists.

"Excuse me?" Jake stared up at the giant ghoul. The green mist swirled around them both, hot and wet.

The street was so silent . . . no cars . . . no voices . . . no rustle of wind in the trees.

Jake could hear his own rapid breathing, hear the thud of his heartbeat in his chest.

"You can't go home, Jake," Johnny Scream repeated, the silver eyes so cold and lifeless.

"Johnny — are you trying to scare me?" Jake asked. His voice sounded tiny, muffled in the choking fog.

Johnny Scream's black suit, patched and torn and many sizes too big, fluttered in the swirling fog, a flapping sound — like a flag in the wind. Or bat wings.

The silver eyes never blinked.

The ghoul's smile revealed two rows of pointed teeth. Sharp spikes.

He clicked the fingernails on his right hand against the fingernails on his left hand in a steady, slow rhythm.

CLICKCLICK CLICKCLICK . . . the only sound now except for Jake's shallow breaths.

"Johnny — why are you trying to scare me?"

Jake demanded. He tried to take a step back. But the fog held him. Pushed against him. Prickled the skin on the back of his neck.

"I'm real, Jake," the ghoul whispered. The patch of cheekbone beneath the open skin glowed green.

"Huh? What are you *saying*?"

"I'm real, Jake. I can't let you go home."

"Johnny, I know you," Jake insisted, unable to keep his voice from trembling. "I know you're not real. You're in my dad's movies."

"I'm not in the movies now," the ghoul replied coldly.

"But you're not real!" Jake declared. "It's all makeup, Johnny. I know it's all makeup!"

With an angry cry, Jake stuck out both hands — and grabbed Johnny Scream's face.

"All makeup!" Jake screamed. And tried to pull off the skin flap. Tried to pull off the ugly mask over the actor's real face.

"Oh!" Jake gasped as his hands stuck to Johnny's face.

His skin was soft — soft and sticky like thick syrup.

Jake tried to tug his fingers free. But they stuck to the soft skin, then stretched it, like taffy, like bubblegum . . .

Jake pulled back — and the sickening, sticky skin kept stretching with him.

I'm stuck! he realized. Stuck to the ghoul's face!

Johnny Scream's eyes gleamed like two beams

of light. His tight, black-lipped smile spread, stretched . . . stretched . . .

And Jake, pulling . . . pulling . . . struggling to free his hands from the rubbery skin, opened his mouth in a horrified scream.

PREPARE TO BE SCARED!